The Stolen Crown

ALSO BY EVA HOWARD

League of Archers

LEAGUE OF ARCHERS

The Stolen Crown

EVA HOWARD

ALADDIN
New York London Toronto Sydney New Delhi

CANCEL

ALADDIN
An imprint of Simon & Schuster Children's Publishing Division
1230 Avenue of the Americas, New York, New York 10020
First Aladdin hardcover edition December 2017
Text copyright © 2017 by Working Partners Limited
Jacket illustration copyright © 2017 by Charlie Bowater
For information about special discounts for bulk purchases, please contact
Simon & Schuster Special Sales at 1-866-506-1949 or business@simonandschuster.com.
The Simon & Schuster Speakers Bureau can bring authors to your live event.
For more information or to book an event contact the Simon & Schuster Speakers Bureau
at 1-866-248-3049 or visit our website at www.simonspeakers.com.
Jacket designed by Jessica Handelman
Interior designed by Mike Rosamilia
The text of this book was set in Adobe Garamond Pro.
Manufactured in the United States of America 1117 FFG
2 4 6 8 10 9 7 5 3 1
Library of Congress Cataloging-in-Publication Data
Names: Howard, Eva, author.
Title: The stolen crown / by Eva Howard.
Description: First Aladdin hardcover edition. | New York : Aladdin, 2017. | Series: League of Archers ; 2 |
Summary: "Ellie Dray and her League of Archers are keeping Robin Hood's legacy alive by stealing
from the rich to help the poor, but when they discover someone is trying to steal the crown, they
learn that some things may be out of their league"— Provided by publisher.
Identifiers: LCCN 2017003330 (print) | LCCN 2017030995 (eBook) |
ISBN 9781481460422 (eBook) | ISBN 9781481460408 (hc) |
Subjects: | CYAC: Robbers and outlaws—Fiction. | Adventure and adventurers—Fiction. |
Characters in literature—Fiction. | Archery—Fiction. |
Middle Ages—Fiction. | Great Britain—History—John, 1199-1216—Fiction. |
Great Britain—History—Henry III, 1216-1272—Fiction. |
BISAC: JUVENILE FICTION / Fairy Tales & Folklore / Adaptations. |
JUVENILE FICTION / Fairy Tales & Folklore / General. | JUVENILE FICTION / Historical / Medieval.
Classification: LCC PZ7.1.H6875 (eBook) | LCC PZ7.1.H6875 Sto 2017 (print) |
DDC [Fic]—dc23
LC record available at https://lccn.loc.gov/2017003330

Special thanks to Melissa Albert

1

A DEAD CHICKEN HUNG INCHES FROM ELLIE'S face, its feet trussed, its body plucked, its blank eye pinning hers. She ducked clear of its gaze, breathing in the pantry smells of blood and dust. Her bow was on her shoulder, an arrow nocked and ready to fly, but she prayed she wouldn't have to use it.

What on earth would Sister Bethan say, she thought, *if I shot a man in the middle of the abbey kitchen?*

Through the crack in the pantry doors she saw Mother Mary Ursula sweeping past, narrow shoulders thrown back in pride. Behind her stood a man whose very presence made Ellie's jaw lock tight and her fists clench: Lord de Lays. The man who had ejected the abbey's beloved mother abbess—after exposing her former life as Maid Marian, companion to Robin Hood and the Merry Men—and framed Ellie for the murder of Robin himself.

The baron had watchful blue eyes set in dark hollows nearly as black as his hair. His round, well-fed face was shaved smooth but for a small, pointed beard he'd grown since Ellie saw him last. She wrinkled her nose at it.

"As you can see, sire," Mother Mary Ursula crooned, "I run the abbey not just on the godly tenets of devotion and service, but on the virtues of cleanliness and discipline." Her voice lingered over the words.

Ellie peered at her through the crack. Mary Ursula's cheeks looked pink and fresh-pinched—or else the presence of the oily-haired baron was actually making her blush.

"And what do you think, Sister Bethan?" the baron asked, his manner as dangerous as a snake in the grass. "Is the abbey much improved since the departure of Maid Marian, traitor that she was?"

Sister Bethan moved in front of the pantry, her back partially blocking Ellie's view. "We have no complaints, sire," she said. Her words sounded like they came through gritted teeth.

"If there's anything else we can do for you, I trust you'll

ask us," Mother Mary Ursula gushed. "We serve at your leave and are always willing to make ourselves useful."

"Thank you, Reverend Mother," he replied. "If you would grant me one thing: your blessing for my journey to Nottingham tomorrow. There I will meet with the other barons of the north—and King John himself."

He paused expectantly, and Mother Mary Ursula rushed to do as he asked.

"May the Lord guide you on the road to Nottingham!" she simpered, with eyes downcast. "May he make your path straight, though it be winding, and may the king be as honored by your illustrious presence as we are." She looked up at him. "How could the king not be pleased? When I was but a girl, my father—a nobleman himself, have I mentioned that?—had occasion more than once to visit the royal court—"

"Yes, yes," the baron said hurriedly. "Thank you for your blessing. I must return to the Castle de Lays before nightfall if I'm to prepare for my journey—but I leave knowing that, through you, God has returned to the abbey at last."

In the darkness of the pantry Ellie bit her lip against a tide of fury. Her own years living at the abbey had revealed Mary Ursula to be gossipy, ill humored, and vain. She was far from godly.

Mother Mary Ursula followed the baron out of the kitchen. With a sigh of relief Ellie let the bow fall from her shoulder, and she was returning her arrow to its quiver as Sister Bethan yanked open the pantry doors. Her face was thunderous.

"Elinor Dray, you had better make sure that's the last attack of the vapors you give me this year!"

Ellie tried to look sheepish as she stepped out into the kitchen. The room was bathed in the golden light of autumn, spilling in over the fire crackling in the hearth, the barrels of grain, and the long wooden table dusted with flour. Through the open window was the green patchwork of the kitchen garden, the air fragrant with thyme and rosemary, then a long stretch of open ground leading to the abbey wall. Beyond that lay Sherwood Forest.

The old nun continued to rage. "Have you forgotten you were made an outlaw on the baron's orders? Ellie, he'd just as soon hang you as look at you—I see you hiding a smile, child, but you won't get one out of me! It's far too risky for you to keep visiting like this—"

"My dear Sister Bethan," Ellie said, her voice tight and prim. "Would you like me better if my father were a nobleman?"

Sister Bethan's lip twitched. "It is unbefitting of a novice nun to tease our new mother abbess."

"Just as well I'm no longer a novice nun, isn't it?"

Sister Bethan gave her a look of great forbearance, then swept her into a hug. "I am happy to see your face, though, child—and grateful for these." She took out a brace of freshly killed rabbits Ellie had handed her when she arrived, secreted from the baron's notice under the wooden table. She put them on the work surface, then cut a slice of bread from a loaf on a wooden board.

"Sit down," Sister Bethan said, ushering Ellie to the table. "And eat this. You're no bigger than a rabbit yourself. You saw the chicken in the pantry, I'm sure—killed this morning for the supper table of the mother abbess and her favorites. Meanwhile, the patients in the hospital live on watery porridge. And any sister faithful to the memory of Marian hardly fares better."

Ellie chewed on the bread, her good humor giving way to frustration. Sister Bethan's words were a reminder that no matter how much she did, it was never enough. Never enough to cancel out the greed of powerful people like Lord de Lays and Mother Mary Ursula.

"I'll come back," she said. Then, seeing the warning flare in Sister Bethan's eyes, "You know I can sneak in unseen. I came in and out a thousand times when I was a novice here."

"And most of those right under my nose," Sister

Bethan said dryly. She took Ellie's chin in her fingers. "I see some mischief cooking behind those eyes, Ellie. As grateful as I always am for your game—and your company—I want you to promise me you'll use the wisdom God gave you to keep yourself safe."

"I promise," Ellie said.

She almost meant it too—but the baron's words about his journey to Nottingham were running through her mind. As she kissed Sister Bethan good-bye and raced across the abbey grounds to the forest, she was already forming a plan.

Nottingham was big, loud, and overwhelming. And it *stunk*. The town's muddy streets were filled with carts bouncing along cobblestones, packs of soldiers, peasants in everything from rags to their Sunday best, and everywhere animals—skinny dogs looking for scraps, horses lifting their tails to add to the stink, cows plodding stolidly through puddles. Merchants sold food and trinkets from stalls, and the whole town had a holiday air.

Ellie stood at the head of her League of Archers: Ralf, her oldest and best friend; his sister Alice; Jacob, who had learned his father's skill of fletching arrows; and Margery, the youngest, whose family owned a butcher's shop and who could skin and gut a rabbit inside a minute. All five of them, outlaws by the baron's decree, were dressed to escape notice. The girls hid their jerkins and leggings—never worn by women, so sure to be remarked upon—with ill-fitting dresses, and all of them concealed weapons under their cloaks. The dust of the road had done the rest, settling onto their hair and skin as they'd made their way from the forest to the town. Now they looked like most of the crowd—country peasants come to Nottingham in the hope of seeing the king.

Ellie yanked at the neck of her dress, which was made for a smaller girl. She'd borrowed it from a villager named Tamsin, who had fled with her family to Sherwood Forest just after midsummer. Ellie's long brown hair was tied in a braid and stuffed under a frilly cap, the kind of thing she never wore.

"Keep your faces hidden," Ellie murmured, "and look out for anyone carrying a heavy purse. You know how badly we need money. And watch you don't get caught! We've got too many people depending on us for that. Margery, Alice, remember: If you *do* get collared, cry. Make them think you're just helpless little girls."

Margery nodded, tucking her red hair inside her cloak. Alice scowled—she hated anyone thinking her less than she was.

Jacob, lanky and blond, raised his eyebrows. "What

about me? You don't think they'd feel sorry for me if I cried?"

"You're about the tallest person in Nottingham," Ralf grumbled. "You're drawing enough attention as it is, without bursting into tears."

"Cry, run, whatever you need to do," said Ellie, "but no weapons if we can help it."

During her fight to clear her name of Robin Hood's murder, Ellie had shed enough blood for a lifetime. It was part of the outlaw's life, and she had killed only to defend herself and her friends. Most days she tried not to dwell on it. But sometimes, at night, the ghosts of those she'd wronged would come to her uninvited.

"Cut their purses off their belts," she said, "then let the crowd get between you before anyone's noticed their money's gone—or seen your face. Let's try to keep in one another's sights."

Ralf pulled up his hood, casting his freckled face in shadow. "What if we get split up?"

"Let's meet back at the Greenwood Tree," suggested Jacob.

Ellie and the others agreed. The Greenwood Tree was deep in the heart of Sherwood Forest and had once been where Robin Hood and his Merry Men made their camp. Sherwood itself had become a camp in recent weeks as villagers fleeing Lord de Lays sought refuge there. Ever since Ellie and her friends outsmarted the baron, freeing Maid Marian from his dungeons just an hour before her execution, he'd been punishing his people for the League's crimes. He'd raised their taxes until they risked starvation if they paid, and imprisonment if they didn't. Ellie and her friends—fine archers, though they were—couldn't hope to feed so many. So Ellie had come up with a new plan. It was one that sang with the promise of true freedom; she was certain Robin Hood would have loved it. She wanted to clear a stretch of land right in the heart of Sherwood Forest, beyond the baron's grasp, and build a farm. If they could set traps around it, making it as protected as the Greenwood Tree, she was sure they could defend it against anyone who managed to stumble upon them—or who sought them out. There they could live as a village of outlaws among the leaves, beyond the reach of Lord de Lays.

All it would take was as many strong backs and willing hands as they could muster. And money—lots of it. It was why the League was in Nottingham.

Ellie dodged elbows and slid between carts, her friends following. Many in the crowd were peasants, but there was a good number of wealthy men and women, too, drunk on ale and excitement, their pockets and purses stuffed full of coins. Ellie and her friends planned to relieve a few of them of those burdens. King John was said to be already inside the castle, and the crowd was thronging toward the road by which he'd leave. And when he did, it was clear what kind of send-off the people of Nottingham had in mind for him.

The League passed a man jabbing his finger at a sack of slimy potatoes his friend was dragging along. "You won't find a buyer for those rotten things."

"A buyer?" his friend scoffed. "These are for King John. I'm going to knock the crown off his head."

The first man snorted. "And get yourself put in the stocks? Besides, your aim isn't that good."

"It'll do him good to get splattered in a bit of potato rot. No more than he deserves. And it'd be worth a whole month in the stocks to see it!"

Ralf nudged Ellie. "And I thought the baron was unpopular," he muttered. "He's got nothing on King John."

Many more were clutching moldy potatoes or wormy apples, ready to fling them at the king. Ellie wasn't surprised. King John was famed for his cruelty.

The League wove through the crowd, eyes peeled for rich pickings. Ellie's eyes were trained on a large man striding beside her, a bag of coins hanging from his belt. She slid closer, until he was almost within reach—then he turned abruptly and was lost among a group of tradespeople.

The League was close to the castle walls, which were almost as tall as an oak tree, with battlements running along the top. At their foot was a strip of grass, and lined up on this were several carriages. Their wooden panels were carved with various coats of arms and polished to a high shine. The horses that had been harnessed to them were munching bales of hay. A group of soldiers stood guard.

Ellie tugged Ralf's sleeve. "De Lays said the barons of the north would be here. Those must belong to them."

Ralf glanced at the carriages, then at Ellie. He raised an eyebrow, and she knew he was thinking the same as her: *There must be something worth stealing inside them. . . .*

The nearest carriage bore a carved unicorn on its side. The soldier responsible for it was fussing over one of the horses, his back turned to the League of Archers. Ellie began sidling up to the carriage.

"Ellie!" whispered Ralf.

She froze. A door in the castle wall swung open just a few paces from where she was standing, and a harried-looking man in a dirty blue jerkin stepped out.

"Right, then," the man called, clapping his hands.

"I'm Master Crump. All those who've been hired to work at the banquet, come with me immediately!"

A steady stream of people emerged from the crowd. They jostled Ellie and her friends as they made their way to the door. Some wore aprons, others carried loads of firewood. One man, clearly a butcher, had a selection of knives rattling in a bag.

A thought struck her.

"The banquet," she said when she'd made her way back to the League. "That's where all the *really* heavy purses will be."

She could almost feel the weight of a bag of coins in her hands, see the farm they could build with them.

Jacob was gaping at her. "What, you think we should break into the castle? Are you mad?"

"He's right," said Ralf. "There'll be five soldiers to every baron in there."

Alice elbowed her brother sharply. "Oh, we can take them on! If we can each manage to steal from a baron or two—"

"No," Ellie said firmly. "We can't all go. Five new servants hiding their faces? Even a baron can't be stupid enough not to notice that. I'll go in alone."

Alice's face fell. Ellie peeled off her cloak and handed her bow and arrows to Ralf.

"Mad," Jacob said again, shaking his head.

"How many servants carry weapons?" Ellie pointed out. "If this is going to work, I've got to look the part." She smoothed down the shabby dress. "Take good care of that," she said to Ralf, nodding at her bow.

"Take care you don't need it." His freckled forehead was creased with worry.

But excitement was bubbling inside Ellie. She turned toward the castle. This was her chance to get all the money they would need for the farm, and more.

"Wish me luck," she said, grinning at her friends. Then she joined the line of people streaming through the door and into Nottingham Castle.

2

THE WOMAN BESIDE ELLIE GASPED WHEN THEY
walked into the inner courtyard. Awed murmurs ran
down the line. Ellie was as impressed as any of them.
Stretched out in the center was a lawn, the grass so green
and neatly clipped that Ellie wondered if even King John
was allowed to walk on it. It was encircled by the soaring
stone walls, the banners that fluttered from them bearing three lions on a scarlet background—the royal coat
of arms, being flown in John's honor. The main body
of the castle, the keep, loomed up ahead. Flags whipped
from the battlements. Rows of windows caught the sunshine. Cut into it too were narrow, vertical gashes—arrow
slits, Ellie knew, designed for archers to fire through.

The line of people following Master Crump jostled one another as they stared at their surroundings. A boy in a dusty cap was gaping so intently he ran into an older man's back.

"Mind your step, boy," the man growled.

Master Crump swung around, annoyed. "Hurry up, you lot. You'll have no time for gawking once you're in the kitchen. The king's cooks will spit on you as soon as look at you if you waste their time on a banquet day."

Ellie kept her mouth shut and her eyes open as they filed into the vast keep. But despite Master Crump's warning, she couldn't help staring at the room they'd entered. It was huge and bright, with fresh straw on the flagstone floor. Above them were arched high ceilings—higher even than the chapel's at Kirklees Abbey—which sent the steady hum of conversation among busy servants and guards echoing around them. Twice Ellie had been in Castle de Lays—once as a prisoner and again to rescue Maid Marian. She'd thought it very grand indeed. But you could fit nearly the whole of the baron's castle into this room alone.

She'd barely had time to take this in before Master Crump hurried them into a gloomy, smoke-smudged passageway. Here their footsteps echoed around the close stone walls, and torches threw wavering shadows over them all. They filed out into another large hall, this one not as massive as before and far less well kept. Rats scuttled from the light of the torch Master Crump took from the wall, and Ellie had to swallow a yelp of surprise when one ran over her foot. *Definitely the servants' part of the castle,* she thought.

Master Crump led them under a high archway, down a brief staircase, and into a warren of passageways crawling with people—servants carrying flagons of ale, piles of cloth or bags of vegetables, and steaming dishes that made her stomach growl. The air smelled of smoke and burned fat. The air grew hotter as they walked, until Ellie longed to tear off the dress that covered her hunting clothes. She had been trying to remember the various turns he took them down, for the purposes of a quick escape later, but realized she'd completely lost track. The inside of Nottingham Castle seemed as tangled as a ball of yarn.

At last they reached the kitchen. When Ellie trooped in after Master Crump, she could hardly contain a gasp.

Years ago, when she first arrived at the abbey after her mother died, she'd been terrified of an illuminated page in Marian's Bible that showed sinners burning in their lake of fire. The kitchen made her think of that picture now. Everywhere were leaping flames, red faces, smoke billowing over meat turning on spits. Servants yelled at one another across open fires, knives flashed over piles of vegetables and slabs of meat.

"Behind you!" a man barked. Just in time Ellie dodged a steaming curtain of water that sloshed from the cauldron he carried.

"Keep sharp," Master Crump snapped. "You're no good to us boiled."

Rapidly he set each new servant to a task—peeling turnips, chopping carrots, scrubbing endless piles of dishes, turning the meat over the fire pits. Ellie shrank into the shadows against the wall, watching the door for a chance to escape. The money she wanted wasn't to be found here but in the banqueting hall—wherever that was. *I could follow one of the servants carrying food,* she thought. *They must be going there. . . .*

Someone grabbed her arm.

She whipped around to see a black-haired woman with a face like a walnut. She pulled Ellie into the middle of the kitchen, where a pile of chickens lay waiting to be plucked. Ellie looked longingly back toward the doorway.

The woman scowled. "Don't tell me you're squeamish."

Her voice was far younger than her looks; her face must have been cooked rough by long years in the kitchen.

"Squeamish?" said Ellie. "Not me."

She grabbed the nearest chicken and began pulling off the feathers. Ellie had plucked plenty of birds, both at the abbey, to help Sister Bethan in the kitchen, and in Sherwood Forest, where Margery would gut and truss them ready for the campfire. Ellie worked quickly, determined to bolt as soon as the chance presented itself.

"Humph. You'll do," said the woman grudgingly.

Another woman, this one as stringy as a runner bean, was talking urgently into Master Crump's ear.

He grunted in annoyance. "Listen up!" he addressed the kitchen. "It seems they're short of servers in the banqueting hall. Not one of you is fit to be seen by the king, but it will be the worse for all of us if the barons wait too long for their feast. Who here can serve without overturning a plate?"

Ellie's heart leaped. This was her chance to get inside the banqueting hall, pouring wine with one hand and fishing for purses with the other.

"I can do it!" she said too loudly.

The runner-bean woman eyed Ellie contemptuously. "I don't think so, Master Crump. She's the dirtiest one here. She'll put the barons off their meat."

Master Crump began turning away. Ellie started forward, alarmed that her chance was slipping away.

"I serve at my father's inn," she said quickly, the lie

slipping like butter off her tongue. "On the road north of Nottingham. I've served far rougher crowds than this one and never spilled a drop."

Master Crump cocked an eyebrow. "Rough, eh? Fine, fine—just follow her." He pointed to the string-bean woman. "Keep your head down, don't drop anything, and above all, hold your tongue."

The string-bean woman looked Ellie up and down, shook her head, then handed her a tray piled with custard tarts. Ellie nearly staggered under its weight, thanking the saints for her strong archer's arms. The tarts smelled like heaven's halls—rich cream and nutmeg, encased in buttery pastry. She gave herself a moment to covet them, then followed the woman out of the kitchen. She could hardly believe her good luck.

The heat and hustle faded behind them. They wound through a few passageways and reached the banqueting hall.

The smell of food, fire, and people hit Ellie like a wave. The hall was so large, minstrels were stationed at each of its four corners, barely audible above the raucous shouts and chatter of the guests. The dishes streamed in endlessly—fruits and cuts of meat heaped high, loaves of bread and sweating rounds of butter, quivering jellies, suckling pigs and roast ducks, whole fish and songbirds you could eat in a bite. The lords and ladies ate from silver platters and drank from golden goblets. They rustled with silks and velvets, the ladies' hair decorated with jewels. Ellie had never seen so much finery in one place. If she could lift just the necklace from the woman nearest her, she could trade it for enough money to buy a pig for every villager.

The tables were arranged in a horseshoe shape. At the head was a glittering throne, built all out of proportion, as if made for a giant. On it sat a man wearing a fur cloak and red velvet robes covered in golden embroidery. Ellie's skin went hot. So this was King John, the monarch so cruel every child could recite a dozen songs and tales about his misdeeds before his or her fifth birthday. His hair was reddish in the torchlight, his face shaved smooth. His cheeks were heavy and smeared with grease from the duck leg he was eating. Ellie's fingers curled around her tray of tarts. For one dark moment she wished she had her bow in her hands instead.

Next to the king, on his right, sat a man in blue with a gaudy gold chain of office, bedecked with flourishes and flowers. *The Sheriff of Nottingham*, she realized. He had been an old foe of Robin Hood and the Merry Men, and seeing him now was like watching a character from a ballad come to life. The sheriff's thick hair and beard were gray, and he darted his eyes to and fro, as alert and cunning as a fox.

The man seated on the king's left was drinking from his goblet, his face hidden. He put the goblet down, revealing hard blue eyes and a pointed black beard. Ellie shivered.

It was Lord de Lays.

All at once the foolishness of her position struck Ellie like a bucket of cold water. Here she was, face hidden by nothing but a layer of dust, half a room away from the man who had made her a fugitive.

What was I thinking? she wondered, aghast.

One thing was certain: She couldn't stay. Not if she hoped to escape Nottingham Castle alive.

Fighting down panic, she started backing out of the banqueting hall, toward the web of hallways that would lead her to freedom. But her path was blocked by the string-bean woman.

"Master Crump should have listened to me," she scolded. "Can't handle it here, can you? Well, you're not leaving until that tray's empty. Those tarts are King John's favorites." She shoved Ellie, sending her swaying a few steps back into the hall. "Go on—go and serve the king!"

Ellie stumbled to the tables. Her hair had gotten loose under the frilly cap, and she let it fall around her face.

She took the tarts to the lords and ladies first, hoping to empty the tray so she could avoid serving King John and standing in arm's reach of Lord de Lays.

Women in silks and men in fur took sloppy handfuls of the pastries, barely looking at Ellie in between bites of food and swigs of wine. As she moved among them, she felt like a moving target, a doe among the trees, the baron's eye the arrow that could bring her down.

"I won't be silent!" roared a voice. It was King John. The eyes of the room turned toward him. His face was red, wine slopping from the goblet he clutched. The sheriff had a hand on his shoulder and seemed to be trying to calm him down. King John slapped it away.

"God's teeth," the king bellowed. "Get off me, man. I don't care who knows it—when I find the thief who dared steal my crown jewels, he'll find himself hanged by sundown."

Murmurs rippled around the room. Even the minstrels stopped playing for a moment.

The crown jewels!

A flame of envy toward the thief ignited in Ellie's chest, along with a grudging respect. The crown jewels were the most valuable treasures in England—the crown worn by the monarch, the orb and scepter he held to show his authority, and dozens of other jewels. They would have been heavily guarded, she knew, and she wondered how the thief had managed it.

"Girl!" It was a woman in a blue gown, snapping her fingers at Ellie. "Are you catching flies or serving sweets?"

Ellie hastily offered the tray to her. The woman helped herself, nibbling the pastry as she continued her conversation.

"If the king can't hold tight to his jewels, however will he hold on to his throne?" She smiled at her companions with the air of a spoiled child used to approval, and was rewarded with their hearty laughter.

Ellie moved on to the next table. Hands decorated with rings plucked tarts from the tray.

"No Englishman would dare commit such a crime," one of the men was saying darkly. "I tell you, this stinks of the French."

"King John is weak," replied his pale, hugely pregnant wife. Her husband put a quelling hand on her arm, darting a look over his shoulder as if the king might be standing behind him.

She shook him off. "Oh, he's too drunk to hear us," she said. "As usual. The French know how little loved he is, and think they can take his place. You mark my words. The next thing they steal will be his throne."

Ellie moved on, so distracted she nearly tipped her

tray into one of the ladies' laps. Usually she cared little about the royal dance of kings and queens that took place far above her head, but what she'd heard had alarmed her. If these guests were right, what might a new ruler mean for the villagers? Would life under a French king or queen be better? Or would it be worse? After all, a new monarch might love food and finery even more than King John and raise taxes higher yet to pay for them. She was sure the lords and ladies of England wouldn't just let France take the throne—there would be a war to defend it. She imagined Ralf and Jacob forced to take up arms, and herself, Alice, and Margery cutting off their hair and following the boys to the battlefield. . . .

Slumped at the next table was a man, nearly as deep into his cups as the king, leaning heavily over a pile of smeared plates. His companions were caught up in a heated conversation over a bet one had made, and nobody's eyes were on their drowsy friend.

Or on the silken purse that hung at his waist, bulging with coins.

Using the tray as a cover, Ellie leaned toward the man, proffering the tarts with one hand while the other nimbly worked at the ribbon that fixed the purse to his belt. The knot gave way. A thrill passed through Ellie as she dropped it into the pocket of her dress.

Now it really is time to go, she thought. Her tray was almost empty and she had a contribution toward their farm. Now if she could get out before the baron saw her, she could call the day a success after all. . . .

"Oi!"

Her heart sank. The string-bean woman was bustling over, as unwelcome as a bad dream.

"Those tarts are almost gone, and you still haven't served the king. Get over there now. You wait until Master Crump hears about this. . . ."

There was nothing for it. Her feet like lead, she made her way to the top table, where King John and Lord de Lays were seated. Her only hope was that the firelight was dim enough, and her face dusty enough, that the baron wouldn't realize the outlaw Elinor Dray was right under his nose.

Up close, King John reeked of drink. His face was red and shiny, his hair damp and stuck to his thick neck. Ellie held out the tray, dipping into a deep bow that she hoped shielded her face from the baron. John swiped clumsily at the tarts in a way that reminded Ellie of a bear pawing up fish from a stream. He bit into one and custard dribbled down his robe.

"Thieves," he growled. Flecks of pastry fell from his mouth. "Thieves who dare steal from their king! When I find them, I'll . . ." He seemed to have trouble completing his thought and reached for his wine goblet instead, taking a long gulp.

Ellie's heart was pounding. Surely she could go now? She turned to make her escape, but the sheriff raised his hand to stop her.

"None for me," he said—but pointed sharply toward the baron, indicating she should serve him next.

The sounds and smells of the room faded away. Ellie felt like she was underwater. Nothing seemed real. She stepped toward her enemy, keeping her hands as steady as she could. All she could hear was the rasp of her own breath, all she could see was the baron's stern profile. . . .

But Lord de Lays was absorbed with watching the king swig noisily from his goblet. His lip curled with distaste and he turned to the man seated on his other side.

"We won't have to put up with this for much longer, Lord Clerebold," he said in a low voice.

"I trust the plan is in place, then?" the man murmured. He was of middle age, with thin gray hair and a monkish look to him.

Despite the danger, despite the foolishness of it, Ellie stood still as a hare, straining to hear the baron's response.

"Indeed," he said softly, his words nearly lost in the

din. "In two days' time the coach will travel by way of the Kirklees road. My men will do the rest."

"And are the . . . the *items* we discussed safe in the meantime? It will not do to have them go missing again."

The baron chuckled. "We couldn't have that, could we?" He clinked his goblet to Lord Clerebold's.

Ellie stood frozen.

The crown jewels, she thought, her heart thumping so hard she thought the men would hear it through her dress. *That must be what they're talking about. The baron is the thief!*

She was brought back to herself by Lord Clerebold looking up at her. She swallowed hard and dipped into another bow, her head as low as she dared. Lord Clerebold glanced at the tray, then waved her away. The baron didn't look up at all.

She turned and walked swiftly toward the door. She felt as light and free as a bird released from a cage. Her mind was racing with what she'd heard. She couldn't wait to tumble her ideas out to the rest of the League, as bright as the gold and silver she'd stolen.

So the crown jewels would be traveling down the Kirklees road—the League's home territory. Anything could cause a cart to break down on that lonely road— a sharp dip in the terrain, an errant stone, five archers in the trees waiting to relieve the baron's men of their ill-gotten jewels. . . . If she and her friends could just steal the jewels away, Maid Marian and Friar Tuck, former Merry Men, would know how to sell them. They wouldn't just make enough money for the farm. They'd have enough to live for years—no, *decades*—out from under the baron's cruel boot.

She was nearly at the door when a terrible sound cut the air. It was something between a gasp and a moan, like an animal caught in a trap. She spun around. Every head was turned toward the top table. Someone dropped a goblet. A woman screamed.

King John was half standing. One brawny hand was propped on the table, the other was clutched around his neck. He was swaying, but not from drunkenness, Ellie thought. Something was wrong. He looked like he'd been pained by bad meat. He groaned again, fingers clawing at his throat, then slumped over the table, eyes and mouth stretched grotesquely wide.

The banqueting hall rang with a din of screams and shouts. Lords rushed to assist the king. One worked his collar loose, while another yelled at a servant to bring water. Lord de Lays was pulling away the king's cloak— and leaning over him to knock away his half-drunk wine goblet with a quick hand, letting the last of the liquid soak into the rushes at their feet. Ellie's eyes narrowed.

King John's gasps faded to a hideous gurgle. With one last convulsion, he fell heavily onto the floor. He lay completely still.

A shocked hush descended on the banqueting hall.

The sheriff straightened up. In a hoarse voice he shouted, "The king is dead!"

3

THE KING WAS DEAD—AND ELLIE WAS CERTAIN
she could identify the murderer. She saw again in her
mind's eye Lord de Lays knocking away John's goblet.

It was poisoned, she thought.

How easy for a man sitting next to the king to slip
something into his wine? Especially given how drunk
John was and how unlikely to notice. She had no doubt
the baron would commit treason—the highest possible
kind—to get what he wanted. His plotting must go far
deeper than smuggling the crown jewels along the
Kirklees road.

Panic swept the banqueting hall. Several ladies burst
into tears. A young nobleman fainted, sending platters

and goblets rolling to the floor. Voices broke out with wild claims.

"He choked on a bone," one woman said. "I would swear it."

"It was a French assassin," a man insisted, his eyes darting around the room as if he would be next. No one was looking toward the baron.

A troop of soldiers rushed into the hall. "Make way!" their leader bellowed as they converged on the body of King John. At the sight of their flashing chain mail, Ellie dropped her tray into the rushes. She had to get out before things got any worse.

Curious servants thronged at the doorway, eager to catch a glimpse of the drama playing out. Ellie pushed her way through them, like a salmon struggling upstream— and a shoulder met hers, sending her spinning. She just had time to see who belonged to the shoulder—a boy a little older than her, dressed in black, his eyes pale blue— before stumbling backward onto the floor.

The purse flew free of her pocket. The gold coins scattered from its mouth, seeming to fly horribly slowly through the air, and showered over her. The boy's blue eyes went wide.

A soldier wrenched Ellie up off the ground, pulling her arm back so hard she gasped. "The king's not paying you that well, servant girl," he said roughly. "What's your name?"

His voice cut through the din. The guests were turning toward this new spectacle, including Lord de Lays.

His face flushed red with anger. "She's the outlaw Elinor Dray! Hold her fast!"

Ellie snapped from her trance. She stamped hard on the soldier's foot and he yelped, his grip loosening just enough that she could wrench free. The doorway was blocked by the throng, so she took off at a dead run for the fireplace.

She had a panicked idea about grabbing a flaming log and fighting with it—just the kind of stupid thing Jacob might suggest—then spied a better weapon. She reached the poker just before the soldier's hands grabbed at the back of her dress, and she swung around and batted him across the face with it. He reared back, roaring.

A baron in a heavy cloak stood between her and a wave of oncoming soldiers, a short sword in his hand. "Stop there!" he commanded, swinging it at her.

She parried the blade away with her poker, sending it flying toward a knot of shocked nobles. Before anyone else could try his luck, she barreled her way to the door.

"Seize her!" the baron yelled furiously.

She squirmed free of the crowd, out of the banqueting

hall at last, and ran. She wove around another troop of soldiers and skidded sharply into a hallway so narrow Friar Tuck wouldn't have fit in it at all.

She sprinted down it, trying to keep her fear in check. She was small, she was quick, and there was just one of her, while the soldiers were heavy with mail and moved in a pack. *I can escape,* she told herself. *I can do it. I just need to find the way out.*

She burst out of the other end of the passageway. The halls seemed endless, flooded with people, all of them yelling or crying or speculating in hushed tones. Word of King John's death had spread through the castle like a plague. Ellie darted through the crowd, moving as quickly as she could without inciting suspicion. Reluctantly she dropped her poker, worried it attracted too much attention.

At first she headed in one direction as much as she could, turning left to make up for every right, assuming she'd reach the end of the castle that way. When that didn't work, she tried to remember features of the halls she'd seen before. Once she stopped to ask a kitchen boy with an ash-covered face to point her toward the court-yard, but he gave her a rude gesture and ran on.

After she passed the same chamber pot twice, panic started kicking in her chest. She was lost, trapped like a rabbit in a warren, the terriers on its heels. She turned, intending to retrace her steps, but a pair of soldiers were sprinting around the last corner.

"There she is!" one shouted, his voice ragged from running.

Ellie's heart lurched. She dashed into the nearest room—a stone-walled chamber with great haunches of beef and pork hanging from hooks in the ceiling. She ran through it, shoving the carcasses as she went so they swung wildly, meat slapping wetly against meat, in hopes that it would delay the soldiers' pursuit. On the other side of the chamber was a door. She burst through it. She was in a passageway with a narrow, circular staircase curving upward at the end. Ellie stumbled toward it, her limbs exhausted. She dragged herself up the stone steps, then swung open the door at the top, and shut and bolted it behind her.

She slumped back against the door, squeezing her eyes shut. She knew she couldn't keep running from the soldiers for much longer.

Think, Ellie, she told herself. *There's got to be another way to escape.*

She looked around her. The room was high ceilinged and filled with warmth from the fire burning in its hearth. Chairs upholstered in rich red velvet were placed around the fireplace, and on the walls hung great tapestries of hunting scenes. Thick furs covered the flagstone floor, and on a polished table was a heap of letters, waiting to be sent, all sealed with a glob of gold wax. Everything was lit by shafts of colored sunlight streaming through the stained-glass windows.

Something shone on the wall above the fireplace: a silver arrow. It was lean and lovely, glinting in the slanting sunlight.

Ellie knew the arrow well. It was an exact match for the one Robin Hood had won from the Sheriff of Nottingham in an archery contest many years ago. She'd carried it in her quiver, just like Robin had, until after they rescued Marian, and she'd given it to her; Ellie had known how much the keepsake of her old love would mean to her. The ballads said that the sheriff had an exact twin of the arrow made and swore to bring Robin down with it, but never made good on his pledge. And now it hung here, on the castle wall.

Ellie looked around the room with new eyes. *These must be the sheriff's private chambers,* she realized.

What would Robin Hood do if he were with her right now? The answer came to her in a giddy burst.

She jumped up on one of the red velvet chairs and lifted the arrow from its fixings. It was light in her hand, the head narrowed to a deadly point.

A volley of fists pounded on the door, sending the latch shuddering. Startled, she nearly fell off the chair. The soldiers had found her.

Time to run again . . .

She leaped down and ripped off her dress, leaving it in a pool on the floor. Light in her jerkin and leggings, the arrow in her hand seeming to restore her energy, she sprinted from the room through a hall lined with suits of armor, up a brief staircase, and into an opulent bed-chamber, its walls painted with murals of various saints at prayer. She ran to the window. The ground was a long way down—too far to jump. To get out, she would have to go back down, which meant fighting her way through the soldiers. And with just one arrow, and no bow, she wouldn't stand a chance.

The sound of running feet reached her. The soldiers had gotten through the door, then.

She ran through more bedchambers, their velvets and silks melting together in a swirl that threatened to suffocate her. She raced through the door and found herself at another spiral staircase.

Thank God, she thought, crashing down it. At the bottom, surely, she would be able to find the courtyard again. . . .

"Got you!" growled a voice. Ellie shrieked. A soldier was at the bottom of the stairs, one hand on his sword.

He lunged toward her. Ellie had no choice but to run back up—and farther away from any chance of escape.

She reached the chamber she'd run out of but could hear the other soldiers within it. If she went back inside, she'd be caught. So farther up the staircase she went, the muscles of her legs screaming, pounding higher and higher up the castle. Through a window she glimpsed the ground, and freedom, ebbing ever farther away.

At the top was a door. She swung it open and staggered inside.

Standing in front of her was the boy with the pale-blue eyes—the one in black, whom she'd knocked into in the banqueting hall. The one who'd seen the stolen purse and heard the baron yell who she was. She saw now that a sword hung from his belt.

He grinned, his eyes gleaming. "I've been looking for you."

"Out of my way," Ellie snarled. She gripped the silver arrow like a dagger and pointed it toward him.

Quick as a cat—quicker than Alice, even—he grabbed Ellie's arm. She tried to wrench free, but he was strong and held her fast. With one black boot he kicked back a tapestry hanging on the wall and dragged her behind it. For a moment she was smothered in the heavy fabric and couldn't see. She struggled violently, but he gave her a shove, and she staggered backward into open space: a narrow alcove in the wall. The tapestry fell back into place, concealing them.

"What," she panted furiously, "in the name of God do you think—"

The boy put a finger to his lips. The sounds of soldiers' boots and booming voices filled the room. They tramped closer, then past the tapestry, and away. Ellie's irritation turned to a confused gratitude.

When the sounds of the soldiers had faded, the boy relaxed against the wall of the alcove. Light filtered thinly through the threads of the tapestry. His features were strong, his gaze clever and quick. His hair was red like Margery's, but with hints of gold and rich brown, like autumn leaves.

He turned his cool blue eyes on Ellie. "Well?" he said.

"Well what?" she asked warily.

"Well, I've just saved your skin." He grinned, and it took the coolness out of his eyes. Ellie just stopped herself from smiling back.

"You did," she replied haughtily. "And thank you. But why help me? Are you hoping for something in return?"

"You're not very trusting, are you, Elinor Dray?"

Ellie scowled. "Life as an outlaw will do that to you." She pushed back the tapestry and went back out into the room. He might have saved her, but no good could come of talking to a boy she'd first seen among the barons, who knew her name and what she was.

The boy followed, drawing the tapestry back into place. In the clearer light she took in his clothes of rich black fabric, covered all over with an embroidered pattern of leaves. The hilt of his sword was unmistakably made from silver.

"It's far easier to be trusting when you live in a castle," she said.

He laughed. "I don't live here, actually. But you're right. I *do* want something. I think you're going to like it."

Elinor raised her eyebrows. She doubted that very much.

He stepped closer to her. She held her ground, watching him through narrowed eyes.

"Look," he said, "I can get you out of the castle. That's more than you can do on your own."

"If you know my name, you know what I can manage on my own," she shot back. "I've done more than escape a few soldiers."

"That's not what I . . ." He rolled his eyes. "This isn't just 'a few soldiers.' Every man in this castle is looking for you, and you're nowhere close to a way out. Do you even know which side of the castle we're on?"

Ellie said nothing.

"I thought not. I'll get you out. I'll save you from the dungeons, or worse."

She folded her arms. "You still haven't said what you want."

"To come with you."

She scoffed at him, trying to hide her surprise. "Come where? I'm an outlaw."

He looked at her solemnly. "I know you are. I want to be one too. I want to join the League of Archers."

Ellie's mouth gaped. *Join* them? This boy with his teasing smile and fancy clothes shouldn't know anything about the League of Archers. Besides, the other members of the League were friends she'd known since she was tiny, and they'd played at being Robin Hood together in the woods. Side by side they'd fought back against Lord de Lays, saved Maid Marian, and chased Will Scarlet through Sherwood Forest. And now this stranger wanted to join them?

And yet . . . what chance did she have of escaping the castle by herself? All she'd done so far was get farther and farther from freedom.

"You're asking too much," she managed. "The League is . . . it isn't looking for new members."

"I'll prove myself," he said immediately, as if he'd expected her to argue. "I'll do whatever it takes."

"But why? You're no outlaw. You're not even a villager. Who *are* you?"

"I'm no outlaw yet. I'm the son of a nobleman." The blue of his eyes clouded over. "The things I've seen—they make me sick. The corruption, the cruelty . . . I know more than you can imagine about the people you're fighting against. I've seen their greed at close quarters, I've grown up with it. Can you say the same thing?"

The boy's anger was as sudden as lightning on a clear blue day. His fists were clenched, the muscles in his face taut. Ellie wasn't sure if it made her trust him more or less.

"No promises," she heard herself say. "But if you get me out of here, we can talk."

"About me joining the League of Archers, you mean?"

"Yes. About you joining the League of Archers."

The boy's anger melted. He was grinning again. "This way, then." He reached for her hand.

Ellie snatched it back. "I can follow you just fine."

"All right."

He hurried away. He was tall, nearly as tall as Jacob, and Ellie had to rush to keep up with his long strides. He walked with ease and familiarity through the bed-chambers, looking straight ahead as he went.

Whoever he is, he knows his way around Nottingham Castle.

The boy led her into a small room with a narrow bed and a large chest. He heaved it open and rummaged around inside, coming up with a length of rope. Ellie kept her face impassive as he turned to grin at her, clearly hoping to catch her looking curious.

Or impressed, she thought with irritation.

He took the rope to a window striped with iron bars. In the middle, two of the bars were missing, creating a space just large enough to fit through. He started tying the rope to one of the remaining bars. Ellie shouldered past him and peered down.

They were at the back of the keep. Below was an empty alleyway, far enough from the crowds that all she heard was birdsong and the breeze.

She narrowed her eyes at the boy. "How did you know where the rope was?"

He shrugged and gave her another infuriating grin.

"How did you know how to find your way to the back of the keep? And how did you know about the League?"

"So many questions," he said, looping the rope in a knot.

"Here's another. You didn't answer me before—who exactly are you?"

"My name's Stephen." He yanked hard on the rope to

test it. "You're the outlaw, not me. Anyway, don't you think this can wait until we're out of the castle?"

Ellie gave a grudging nod.

Stephen smirked and gestured toward the window. "Good. Now, who's going down first?"

4

ELLIE LOOKED FROM STEPHEN'S SMUG FACE TO the sheer drop to the alleyway below. "After you, I think."

"As you wish."

Not quite believing he'd do it, Ellie watched Stephen wrap the rope around his fist and swing first one leg, then the other, over the window ledge. The sun lit up his bright hair as he braced his feet against the wall and stepped his way, bit by bit, down the sheer stone. Ellie leaned out to watch his descent. When he was close to the alley, he leaped down and grinned up at her.

Ellie hesitated for a moment. It was a very long way down.

Come on, she told herself. *It's this or take your chances with the guards.*

So she wrapped one fist with rope, as Stephen had done, and levered herself out into the open air.

It was nothing like being in the Greenwood Tree, she reflected. If she stepped wrong in the Merry Men's hideaway, now the adopted base of the League of Archers, it was a long drop, but she never felt in danger there. She always felt protected by the ingenious walkways—first built by Robin and his men, later patched up by the League—by the arms of the tree, and by the benevolent spirit of the place.

But now, rappelling down Stephen's rope, if she maneuvered wrong, let her hand slip, she'd plummet to the ground. The stone wall was rough through her boots, the rope murder on her palms. She went down hand over hand, keeping her eyes trained on the rope, not daring to look down at Stephen in the alley below.

"You can let go now, I'll catch you," he called when she was almost at the bottom.

She ignored him, jumping her own way down to solid earth. "Thank the blessed saints," she murmured, rubbing her sore hands.

"Thank me, not the saints," said Stephen. "I'm the one who got you out. I hope you're a girl of your word."

"We're out of the castle, not out of danger. Come on— the rest of the League will be wondering what's happened to me. Don't do anything to draw attention."

She could hear the Nottingham crowd once more. It grew louder as they made their way out of the alley and into the town's streets. But the tenor had changed—before, there had been music and shouts, and a festival feeling in the air. Now the people sounded like an angry mob—and looked like one too. They were packed shoulder to shoulder in the street, their faces twisted with concern, anger, and fear. One phrase kept ringing out above the hubbub: "The king is dead!"

Bad news spreads fast, Ellie thought grimly. Had word spread too of the girl running from the scene of his death—the outlaw Elinor Dray? If Stephen had remembered her face, others would too.

They joined the bustling throng, Ellie peering around in the hopes of spotting lanky Jacob's sandy-colored head above the rest. Stephen kept close beside her. They pushed past a man wearing a bloodstained apron who looked like he'd run to join the crowd straight from his butcher's shop.

"What's going on?" the butcher was asking a woman wrapped in a tattered shawl.

"There's been a fight among the barons," she said with certainty. "And when the king's friends fight, it's worse for us somehow."

"No," joined in another woman, who was holding a

red-faced baby to her chest. "I heard it was a surprise attack. The king was set on by a French lord hiding in a suit of armor."

"That'll come down on our heads too," the butcher replied darkly. "You can be sure of it."

The rumors got wilder as they went. "That French wife of his is to blame," a woman in a filthy apron told her friend. "The king learned of her plot to run off with a baron and make a fool of him."

"Well, I heard the king cast her out—he's going to marry a Spanish princess instead."

Stephen snorted. "That's so ridiculous!"

The two women stared at him. "I suppose you know better, young man?" snapped one, her eyes narrowed.

"Maybe I do," said Stephen.

Before he could say more, Ellie grabbed his arm and yanked him away.

"What do you think you're doing?" she whispered. "We're trying not to get spotted, remember?"

"Like your friends, you mean?" He waved an arm at the crowd. "Let's face it, you're never going to find them in all these people."

He was right, Ellie realized. And the rest of the League must have guessed how impossible it would be for Ellie to reach them again. They were probably on their way to the Greenwood Tree—and the sooner she followed them, the better. It surely wouldn't be long before soldiers spilled out of the castle, shouting her name and ordering her captured. But what would her friends say when she turned up with a stranger in tow?

I could lose him here, she thought. *Just slip away in the crowd. It would be as easy as a deer disappearing into the trees.*

She glanced around, readying to dash away—and saw that Stephen was looking at her expectantly. She sighed. She couldn't do it. She'd given her word—her word as the leader of the League of Archers. He'd kept his side of the bargain, and now she had to keep hers.

"You're right," she said. "They're not here. We'll meet them at the Greenwood Tree."

His pale-blue eyes went wide. "The Greenwood Tree? You mean the one where Robin—"

"Keep it down!" she snapped. "Yes, that one, of course. Let's hurry, before it gets dark."

They struggled through the crowd. Everyone else seemed to be surging toward the castle, as if they thought they could figure out its secrets just by gathering before its walls. Ellie thought of the dead king inside, his body growing cold. John had been a cruel ruler, but surely even he hadn't deserved such a painful end. She thought too of Lord de Lays and the malice in his face when he saw her across the hall. What would his next move be? He'd killed the king and he already had the crown jewels. Did he plan to wear the crown himself and sit on England's throne?

At last they left the crowd behind. The narrow town streets gave way to fields and muddy lanes. As they turned onto the road that led to Sherwood Forest, Ellie inhaled deeply, glad to breathe in the scent of earth and grass once more.

She glanced at Stephen, who strode along with the swagger of a lord surveying his estate.

"We've got time for those questions now, haven't we?" she said.

"Go on, then."

"How do you know Nottingham Castle so well? And don't try to tell me you're a servant."

"Why would I do that? I've already told you my father's a nobleman. We visit the castle sometimes." He squared his shoulders, as if daring her not to believe him. "My father is friends with the sheriff. He had a hand in organizing the banquet."

"I don't think it went exactly as he planned."

He gave a surprised laugh. "No, I suppose it didn't. But at least the king isn't around to complain."

Ellie had no love for King John, but she was a little

shocked at this. She could just imagine Sister Bethan's face if she heard Stephen mocking the dead. She hardened her voice. "You'll find it's much tougher staying in the forest than at a castle."

"I'm sure," said Stephen breezily.

"How do you even *know* about the League, anyway?"

He shrugged. "How did anyone know about the Merry Men? People talk. You and the League stand for something. Which is more than my father can say."

"What does your father have to do with it?"

"I hate him," he said. His blue eyes flashed again with the anger he'd shown earlier. "I'd rather be an outlaw than live with him. I'd rather sleep in the dirt and . . . and eat nothing but twigs and berries than live with him."

Ellie couldn't understand it: to hate your family so much you'd leave them behind. She hadn't seen her father since he left her and her mother years ago to join the Crusades. As far as she knew, he'd died there. In his absence the baron had seized the Dray home, so Ralf and Alice's family had taken Ellie and her mother in. Desperate to earn their keep, Ellie's mother had hunted on the baron's land—and when she was caught carrying home a deer, the baron had had her hanged.

Ellie missed her parents all the time. Some days it was

LEAGUE OF ARCHERS

like a scream she couldn't voice, but most days it was an ache. A beat of sorrow that lived inside her heart. If they had been alive, she couldn't imagine turning her back on either of them, no matter what. Stephen must surely have good cause to leave his father behind.

She gave him a nudge. "Don't worry. We manage better food than twigs. And the dirt's actually pretty comfy."

His face softened somewhat.

"But are you sure about this? What could your father have done to make you leave home? Surely things can't be that bad."

"Not that bad?" Just like that, his anger returned. His brows, much darker than his hair, drew into a scowl. "You don't know what you're talking about."

"All right, calm down! Sorry I asked."

They strode on. Ellie searched around for something to say that would lighten the mood, but she couldn't think of anything.

At last Stephen broke the silence. "He did something terrible. Something that can never be put right. That's why I want to join the League." There was no bite to his words—he just sounded sad.

In the chill light of early evening Ellie led Stephen off the road and over windblown fields. When they reached the edge of Sherwood Forest, she stopped Stephen and unwound the black scarf he wore around his neck. He raised an eyebrow.

"You're wearing a blindfold," she explained. "The way to the Greenwood Tree is secret to everyone except the League of Archers."

"But I'm joining the League," he protested.

"You're not a member yet. I'm leader of the League, not their king—we make our decisions together. You're not in unless all of us decide you're in."

"Fine," he grumbled.

She covered his eyes with the scarf, tying it tight behind his head. "Now give me your sword."

"You're joking."

"I'm not."

He grunted before carefully drawing the blade, passing it to her, hilt first. She grasped the beautifully carved handle and tucked it into her belt.

The rest of their journey took far longer than it should have. Leading Stephen was like leading a balky pig. Ellie had to guide him around trunks and through the underbrush, help him up when he stumbled, and ignore his complaints that she should just let him take off the blindfold. They splashed through the chilling, waist-deep water of a river because Ellie judged it impossible to lead a blindfolded boy over the narrow bridge Jacob had built to span it. Stephen winced as blackberry brambles snatched at his clothes, and swore when he walked into a face full of pine needles.

But their journey became far more perilous when they reached the dangerous ground around the Greenwood Tree. There they had the Merry Men's traps to contend with, repaired and reset by the League of Archers. Despite Ellie's orders, Stephen got cocky and put on a burst of speed, nearly tumbling over the edge of a pit trap.

She tackled him to the grass and yanked up the blindfold. He had the grace to look chastened at the sight of the large hole he'd almost fallen into, which was lined with sharpened spears like a dragon's teeth.

"Exactly," she reprimanded him. "So don't think yourself clever. Out here, with our traps, you're as ignorant as a donkey."

He was easier to lead after that, following her commands to the letter. At last they reached the thickly clustered greenery at the edge of the clearing where the Greenwood Tree grew, and where the League made their camp. She could hear the murmur of voices and smell smoke from the campfire. It struck her forcefully what she was about to do—expect their close-knit group to accept a stranger she'd met a bare few hours ago.

I had to let him come, she thought. *It was that or be captured. They'll understand, won't they?*

It was time to find out.

She took Stephen's arm and pushed through the thick wall of greenery and into a clearing.

Ralf was the first to notice her, looking up from where he sat sharpening their knives against a whetstone.

"It's Ellie!" he cried, his voice ringing with relief. "She's made it back!"

He started to stand—then saw Stephen, grappling his blindfold free, and froze.

"About time!" Alice cried, her voice coming from high in the Greenwood Tree. "Ellie, we were starting to worry!"

Stephen looked up in wonder at the tree's leafy expanse, full of platforms and walkways and tiny wooden rooms. The League still lived mainly in the arms of the tree, but Jacob had put up a tent on the other side of the trunk to sit in when he made arrows—he loved heights less than the rest of them—and he emerged from it now. When he saw Stephen, a clutch of arrow shafts fell from his hand. By the crackling fire Margery sat, paused partway through skinning a deer to stare at the stranger. The flames cast dancing shadows across the shocked faces of the League.

Alice, climbing down the tree, was the only one who hadn't noticed him.

"We were starting to think you wouldn't get out," she was saying. "People were running in and out of the castle, the soldiers were trying to push them back—we wanted to wait, but we knew you'd never find us." She jumped to the ground and pushed back her untidy curls. "So what exactly happened . . ." Her voice faltered to silence.

Ellie gestured toward Stephen.

"He helped me escape," she explained. "The guards had me surrounded. I'd be in the dungeons now if it weren't for him. He . . . I promised him something in return, if he got me out of the castle." *Just say it.* "I . . . I told him he could *maybe* join the League of Archers. If we all agree to it."

Alice's mouth dropped. Margery stood up sharply from the fire. Jacob marched toward Ellie, the anger on his face making her stomach drop.

"Ellie, you've been tricked," he said, his voice like ice. "He hasn't come to join the League. He's come to ruin us."

Ellie gaped at him. "Ruin us?"

Jacob nodded grimly. "This is Stephen de Lays. The baron's son."

5

HE CAN'T BE, THOUGHT ELLIE, HER MIND A whirl of confusion. But when she studied Stephen's face, she at last saw the truth of it: His cool blue eyes, the sharp cheekbones beneath them, exactly like his father's. His hair sweeping back from the baron's high forehead, the arrogant cast of his shoulders.

Oh, how could I have been so foolish?

Jacob had seized a bow and quiver of arrows from where they were propped against the trunk of the Greenwood Tree. He nocked an arrow to the bow, training it on Stephen. Stephen's face turned pale, but he lifted his chin and looked Jacob in the eye.

"I'd know you anywhere," Jacob said, his voice rigid

with an anger Ellie had never seen in him—not when the baron took Maid Marian, not when he was made an outlaw and had to leave home. "I was with my father on the last tax day. I saw *your* father demand more money, more than we'd ever given. And I saw you sitting right there beside him, smiling when he told you what a good lesson this was—a lesson in keeping the peasants in their place!"

"I wasn't smiling," Stephen said. His voice was low and steady. "I hate him as much as any of you—I know the taxes are wrong; they're cruel, but if you'd just listen—"

"No baron's son can ever join the League of Archers," said Ralf, moving to Jacob's side. Alice went with him, her face as fierce as the knife she'd snatched up.

Stephen swallowed. "Please don't kill me. Just *listen*."

Ellie saw Jacob's fingers tremble on the bow, realized his anger might make him clumsy. Swiftly she moved between Stephen and her friends. Jacob growled but lowered his bow.

"Of course we're not going to kill you, Stephen. Are we?" she said sharply to the League. "That's not what we do. But Ralf and Jacob are right—the baron's son can't join us. You're putting the blindfold back on and we're leaving the forest. Now."

Stephen shook his head. "I meant everything I told you. I'm not going back."

"You *tricked* me!" The words burned on the way up. "You're a liar and your father's spy. Whose idea was it for you to *save* me, yours or his?"

Stephen's sword still hung from her belt. Ellie drew it. If she had to force him to leave, so be it.

For the first time Stephen looked afraid, but he stood his ground. "I would never help that man. You must believe me. He's no father to me—he never has been. His cruelty to me, to my mother . . ." His voice was unsteady. "I'm the last person in England who would help Lord de Lays. I want revenge for what he did."

"What did he do?" Margery's voice held the barest rind of sympathy.

"Killed my mother, or as good as. Blamed her for not producing more sons, hated the one he had, and let her lie with a fever three days after my sister was stillborn. Mother was the only person who . . . she was the only . . ." His eyes filled with the sadness Ellie had seen on the road through the woods. "After she died, he sent me to the Crusades. I was a squire, serving a knight, barely eleven years old. I saw terrible things in the Holy Land. Terrible." His eyes locked on Ellie, stern under storm-dark brows. "That's what my father did."

She stared back, still seeing the baron in his face but noticing the differences now too. His nose was narrower than his father's, the bones of his face more pronounced. She tried to imagine the woman who had married de Lays and produced Stephen. How his cruelty would have made her a prisoner. How much colder their castle must have become for Stephen after she died.

"I want the same as you," Stephen said. "To make him pay. And I know more about him than you ever could. Can't you see how useful I'd be to you?"

Ellie's head was swimming. "We don't want to make the baron pay," she said shortly. "We want to help the poor."

"I want that too," Stephen said eagerly.

"How do we know he's not lying?" Alice's voice sounded rusty.

"We don't," Ellie replied.

"Then I think we should tie him up. Till we figure it out."

"What's there to figure out?" Jacob asked. His bow was lowered, but still taut and ready to fire. "He's the baron's son."

"I never chose to be," countered Stephen. "No more than you choose to be his subject."

Ellie turned away. Of course Stephen hadn't chosen his father. *But does that even matter?* He'd grown up at his father's table. He'd never known hunger, never known true want. Yet he had also saved her from certain capture.

If not for him, she'd be shivering in a cell right now. Or hanging from a gallows. And she was sure his being here was no plot—neither the baron nor his son could have known Ellie would be in the castle that day. She hadn't known it herself.

The clearing had fallen silent, her friends looking to her to decide what would be done with him. She was the leader, and she'd brought Stephen de Lays here, to the very heart of the League. Alice watched her with narrowed eyes, Margery with wide ones. Jacob still held his bow taut, as if ready to shoot the moment Ellie gave the word.

Ellie's eyes met Ralf's, and a wordless agreement passed between them. She knew he saw what she did—that the situation was more complicated than Jacob allowed. Who was she to claim to read Stephen's mind, to know his true intentions? She knew now what her decision must be.

"You can stay."

Alice gave a disappointed hiss and Jacob threw down his bow in disgust. Ellie ignored them both.

"But," she said, stepping closer to Stephen, "if you give us even the *slightest* reason for doubt, you're gone."

"Or worse," Alice muttered.

Relief flooded Stephen's face. "Thank you," he said. "You won't regret it. I swear I'll make you glad I'm in the League."

He would have said more, but Jacob stopped him. "Go over there," he said rudely, gesturing toward a corner of the clearing. "I need to talk to our leader."

Stephen shot a look at Ellie but did as he was told. She remembered what she'd told him earlier: "I'm the leader of the League, not their king—we make our decisions together." Yet she'd been the one who'd ruled that Stephen could stay, ignoring Jacob's and Alice's objections. Wasn't that the behavior of a king? The thought gave her a quicksilver flash of shame. She rubbed her eyes. What else could she have done? Even Robin Hood had had to decide what was best for his Merry Men.

Of course, in the end his Merry Men had left him.

Jacob's jaw was tight. "I'll watch him, Ellie. I'll watch his every move. If he does anything that doesn't seem right—I'll see it first."

"Good idea," she said, wondering what on earth she'd done.

That night felt like it stretched on forever. Every time Ellie's eyelids started to droop, she jolted back to waking, remembering the intruder in the clearing. The intruder *she'd* brought in.

Not an intruder, she corrected herself. *Stephen.*

Still, she reached her fingers out in the dark and

felt better when they wrapped around the hilt of his sword. It lay safely beside her on her platform high in the Greenwood Tree, next to her bow and arrows. Alice and Margery, lying near her, stirred restlessly. She could see Ralf's profile where he sat on a nearby platform; he clearly couldn't sleep either. And when she peered down through the leaves, she could see the fire still smoldering below, Jacob huddled beside it. His bow and arrow were at his feet, his eyes fixed on where Stephen lay sleeping beneath his cloak on a heap of dried leaves.

Someone's getting a good night's rest, she thought resentfully.

The next day everyone went about their business without talking. Alice disappeared early to hunt, Margery settled down to skin rabbits, and Ralf took over watching Stephen so Jacob could climb up into the tree's branches to sleep. Stephen mostly kept out of their way. He leaned cross-legged against the roots of the Greenwood Tree, staying quiet, awkward as an uninvited guest. Which, Ellie supposed, he was. Finally Ralf took pity on him, handing him a rabbit carcass and a knife to skin it with.

"You're giving him a knife?" Jacob said incredulously, climbing blearily from the tree.

"Why not?" Ralf said. "It's not like he can *do* anything with it."

Stephen flushed, and Ellie could see he was biting back

a response. He applied himself with enthusiasm to the rabbit, making a mess of it, until Margery stepped in and firmly took it away.

"Well, skinning's right out. What *can* you do?" she said.

"Oh, sharpen knives, fletch arrows, whittle pretty much anything," he said airily. "I wasn't a squire for nothing, you know."

"You were really in the Crusades?" Jacob said, his voice sounding almost impressed. Then he cleared his throat, making his face indifferent. "You can't have done much fighting, though. My father says most of the crusaders just spend their days wading through muck."

"And blood. We spent our days wading through muck and blood."

Jacob stood awkwardly for a moment, then handed Stephen a clutch of branches. "Here," he said abruptly. "You say you can whittle—these need to be made into arrow shafts."

They left him to it. When the sun was at its highest, Ellie brought Stephen a skin of water. As he gulped it gratefully, she sat beside him. There was a pile of arrow shafts at his feet, almost as neat as Jacob's.

"We've been talking," she said. "We want to show you something."

"Okay."

"It's something . . . well, your father wouldn't like it. We're trusting you with a secret."

"I swear you can trust me. And if my father wouldn't like it, that means I will."

So the League led Stephen, his blindfold back on, through the trap-laden forest to an area cleared of trees. What had started as a space not much larger than the abbey's kitchen had already grown into something the size of a small village. On one side was the beginnings of their farm—chicken coops, a fledgling vegetable garden, some pens intended for sheep and cows. On the other was a clutch of small shelters, some complete, some just bare wooden frames. Men and women hoisted the beams for a new shelter, while children wove together sticks and branches for the walls, then slapped on handfuls of heavy clay to complete them. The pride of the camp was the Baker family's tiny shop front. It was a neat, timber-framed building, looking nearly as it had in the Kirklees village. Two women stood outside, hair wet with sweat from their labors, but they were smiling as they gossiped.

Ellie untied Stephen's blindfold and he gaped at the scene. "What is this place?" he breathed.

"Just what it looks like," said Ellie proudly. "New homes for everyone fleeing your father's taxes and a farm to feed them."

Jacob and Margery went to help the villagers raising beams for the shelters. Ralf and Alice went to speak to a blond girl putting the finishing touches to one of the chicken coops. She was called Cecily, Ellie remembered, and had been a neighbor of Ralf and Alice's before the baron made them outlaws and they had to leave the village. Now Cecily must have been forced to leave too.

Ellie realized that it wasn't just Cecily who was new. There were far more people in the clearing than there had been even a week ago. And today, for the first time that autumn, there was a bite in the air that meant the year would soon turn to winter.

We need to get this place ready before then, Ellie thought. *There's no point in these people fleeing the baron only to die of cold.*

Friar Tuck was overseeing an outdoor oven made of bricks, a fire inside it and a vat of bubbling liquid on top. The unmistakable smell of brewing beer reached Ellie. His tonsured head was bent over it, the bald patch on top reddened by the sun, his brawny arms stirring the beer with a vast spoon. Maid Marian, her hair in a thick silver braid, dipped a tankard into the beer and sipped. She gave an approving nod.

"Stay here," Ellie told Stephen. "Just don't do anything. Or," she threw back over her shoulder, "you can help Jacob and Margery!"

Marian smiled when she saw Ellie, velvety eyes soft over her elegant cheekbones. Friar Tuck stopped stirring the beer. "How did it go in Nottingham?" he asked. "Were the pickings good?"

Ellie thought with a pang of the gold-filled purse that had almost been hers, until she dropped it fleeing the banqueting hall. She shook her head with regret. "We'll try again, though. Soon."

"I worry it won't be soon enough." Marian looked around the clearing, her face creased with concern. "If we can't get enough shelters built, enough food in the ground or in storage, I don't know how we'll all make it through the winter."

"True enough," said Tuck. He nudged Ellie. "Now, tell us all about what *did* happen in Nottingham. I know you too well to believe that it wasn't an adventure."

So Ellie did. She beckoned to the rest of the League to come and listen—in all the wrangling over what to do with Stephen, she'd not told them what had happened in the banqueting hall. Their eyes widened with shock as she described the death of King John.

"You're certain it was murder?" Friar Tuck asked grimly. "The man didn't choke on his own greed?"

"It was poison, I'm sure of it."

"The murder of a king won't be good for any of us,"

Marian said. "Trouble will stretch farther than we can imagine."

"I'm sure the baron killed him," Ellie said. "The way he knocked over the cup—I know it was him. And there's something else I need to tell you too." She described the escape from the castle, ending with the revelation about Stephen.

"Stephen de Lays," said Marian. "Yes, I remember him. I met him once, at the abbey—he was younger then, his father's small shadow." Her eyes were touched with pity. "Perhaps if you want to know more about the baron's plot, you could ask the one person here who truly knows him."

Ellie looked to where Stephen sat on a heap of wood, long legs stretched out in front of him. She called him over. He came slowly, as if he were in trouble. When Ellie introduced Marian and Tuck, his eyes grew round as chestnuts. Ellie hid a smile. *Maybe it isn't just village children who play at being Robin and his Merry Men,* she thought.

She repeated her story to him. He listened in silence, face as still as a mask.

"So your father killed King John," Ellie finished. "Don't try to deny it—I know what I saw. But *why* did he do it? Is he helping the French? Does he want the throne for himself?"

"I don't believe it," Stephen muttered. He ran his hands through his bright hair. "I mean, I *do* believe what you said—I just never thought my father would go that far. Killing the king! My God."

"But why did he do it?" pressed Alice.

Stephen gave a bitter laugh. "How should I know? He's ambitious. He'll get something out of it."

"We know he's helped the French before," Ralf said. "Maybe he's helping King Louis take the throne."

"The only person he ever helps is himself," said Stephen bitterly. "If he *is* working for Louis, it'll be in exchange for land, or a title, or gold. Mark my words."

No closer to figuring out the baron's plot, the League went to help finish constructing a shelter large enough to hold two families. Stephen threw himself into the work, taking the heaviest loads, attacking the gnarled stumps that needed to be dug up to make way for the new house. He worked until he was sweaty and panting, yet it made Ellie uneasy. She believed him when he said he hated his father, but she still wasn't sure it made him right for the League. Surely a person needed to be driven by more than just revenge to do something good in the world.

When the shelter was done, Alice tied Stephen's blindfold back on—a little too tight, it looked like—and the rest of the League led him off through the lengthening dusk, back toward the Greenwood Tree.

Ellie lingered behind. She needed advice and hoped Maid Marian could give it to her. She'd loved Marian ever since she knew her only as the mother abbess. Marian had come to collect Ellie from the village after her mother was hanged, taking her in at Kirklees as a novice nun. At first Ellie loved her with the blind devotion of a grieving orphan, desperate for someone to care for her. Later, when she discovered Marian's true identity, she loved her with a fierceness born of knowing how truly good and brave Marian was.

Friar Tuck, on his way back to the beer, ruffled Ellie's hair. "Is the Greenwood Tree taking good care of you?"

"Always. And we're taking good care of it, too."

Many of the tree's more ingenious devices were the friar's doing. His eyes always shone when Ralf showed him the bits they'd patched up or even improved, though he rarely took them up on their offer to stay with them in the clearing. It was too full of ghosts for him and Marian—ghosts of Robin, of Will Scarlet, Little John, and the rest of the Merry Men.

Marian put an arm around Ellie and led her to a stack of logs behind the row of shelters. Lanterns peppered the approaching dark, and they could hear the friendly sounds of families talking, eating, settling down for the evening.

"Something's troubling you, isn't it?" asked Marian, sitting on one of the logs and drawing her skirts around her—Lincoln-green skirts, the color worn by the Merry Men.

"It's Stephen," she replied. Marian waited patiently while she sat beside her, ordering her thoughts. "It's just . . . I truly believe he won't betray us to the baron. Anyone can see how much he hates his father, and I don't blame him. But have I done the right thing, letting him stay?" She gestured around at the clearing, at the shelters, at the families huddled together breaking bread. "I've just got this awful feeling I've put everything in danger."

Marian took Ellie's hand. "You've done the right thing: You kept your word." She smiled at Ellie's relief. "Everyone deserves a chance, don't you think? You've given Stephen his. It's up to him now what he does with it."

Ellie grinned. "Thank you," she said. "You always make me feel better."

After a little while she left Marian and set off for the Greenwood Tree. As she strode through the shadowed forest, a plan formed in her mind, as clear as the cool night air. She knew now how to get the new farm built by winter.

Tomorrow the crown jewels would be traveling down the Kirklees road.

And the League of Archers is going to steal them!

6

THE LEAGUE OF ARCHERS WERE CROUCHED IN
the trees beside the Kirklees road, looking out for the
coach carrying the crown jewels. When she glanced at her
friends, Ellie saw that Jacob's eyes weren't on the road,
but on Stephen. He'd barely let Stephen out of his sight
since he joined the League. Last night Jacob had slept in
the roots of the Greenwood Tree so he'd hear if Stephen
tried taking off in the night. During every daylight hour
he'd been Stephen's shadow, whether he was fletching
arrows, skinning game, or making plans with the rest of
the League.

Ellie sighed. *How long is this going to go on?*

She wondered if they would ever be able to truly trust

Stephen, and supposed that today's mission was as good a test of that as any. She still cursed the loss of the purse of gold in the banqueting hall, but if they could seize this quarry, her ill-fated trip to the castle—and Stephen's presence at the Greenwood Tree—would all be worth it. They'd be able to feed the villagers for years.

From the branches overhead came the call of a thrush—Margery, keeping lookout. Ellie edged toward the road. As soon as she saw the coach coming toward them, she knew it was their target. It was made of a lovely pale wood, with grilles over the windows to block anyone from seeing inside. Surrounding it were eight men on horseback, clad in helmets and chain mail, swords swinging at their belts. The dark-haired man leading the charge wore a velvet cloak the color of spring leaves. To anyone else on the road it would have looked like a transport for some rich lord or lady. But Ellie knew the truth: The men were there to protect the crown jewels.

"That's the one," she hissed to the League.

Margery dropped down beside them. They all raised their bows to their shoulders, arrows ready to fire. Stephen had a bow too, one of the extras Ralf had made since leaving the village, and his sword was back at his belt. "You'd better not try anything," Jacob had warned him that morning when Ellie handed back the blade. Ellie had seen something rise in Stephen's eyes—a quick flash of irritation—but he'd simply nodded in agreement.

He was straight and alert now, watching the oncoming coach and its guards. Something in the way he held himself told her he'd done more than squire while he was away at the Crusades.

"Fan out," Ellie murmured. "Draw."

They spread out in an arc, bowstrings pulled back, arrows at the ready. The coach rattled closer. Ellie could feel the tension in the air thickening.

"Eight guards," Ralf whispered. "Eight against the six of us."

"We have surprise on our side," Ellie said. She kept her voice firm, but with every moment the coach drew closer, her body felt more taut than her bowstring. She forced herself to breathe steadily, played out what would happen in her mind: They would overcome the men, they would steal the jewels, they would give hope and food and shelter to every peasant fleeing the baron's grip.

The coach was very close now. She could see the soldiers' eyes gleaming under their helmets, make out the flies buzzing around the horses. It was time.

"On my count," she whispered. "One, two, THREE!"

She burst out onto the road. The League flanked her,

all of them training their arrows on the men surrounding the carriage.

The horses reared back. The guards swore. "What's the meaning of this?" cried the man in green, pulling the reins of his bucking horse, its hooves kicking up dust.

"Stop there!" Ellie cried. "Raise your hands or we'll shoot!"

For a long, thin moment she thought they'd refuse her. Then the green-cloaked leader gave a terse nod, and sixteen hands went into the air. Her heart speeding in her ears, Ellie walked toward the coach door, her arrow still poised to fly.

The sizzle of a sword being drawn stopped her short. It belonged to the man in green.

"If you value your life," he said, "you'll step away from that door."

Ellie paused, just a split second too long—and the man gave a short jerk of his head.

In the space of a breath everything changed. The seven remaining men drew their swords and, with a wild chorus of yells, charged toward the League. The guard nearest Ellie swept his blade in a broad arc that would have caught her wrist if she hadn't twisted away, firing her arrow before his horse's eyes so the animal skidded back in panic.

Another man yelled and dropped his sword as Ralf loosed an arrow into the unprotected spot under his arm, then he jumped off his horse and tried to grab Ralf before he could string another arrow. Ralf swung his bow wildly, before the riderless horse reared up and came down heavily on the man's shoulder, knocking him to the ground.

Ellie shot three arrows in quick succession, hitting two men in their sword hands and a third in the leg, just before he swung on Margery. She spared a glance for Stephen, stringing another arrow in the middle of the fray, then dived aside as a guard on horseback bore down on her. She saw a flash of heavy teeth and wild eyes before rolling clear.

Up on her feet again, she restrung her arrow and swung it back and forth among the guards still on their horses. She'd killed two men in battle before. Sometimes their ghosts joined that of her mother, visiting her memory on the nights she couldn't sleep. She had no wish to add another dead man to her conscience, but this was starting to feel desperate.

The man in green was off his horse, his thin face set. He strode toward Jacob and parried the bow, knocking it from his hands in one ferocious sweep. Jacob staggered to the ground and the man stalked closer. Ellie's fingers were slippery with sweat; they fumbled as she nocked another arrow.

Too late. The man was pulling his sword arm back, ready to make a killing blow.

"No!" came Margery's horrified shriek.

Stephen was running toward the man and Jacob. He threw aside his bow and drew his sword, and as the green-cloaked man swung his blade, Stephen met it with his own. They smashed together in a clang and scrape of metal. The man gave a yell of surprise. Stephen whirled his sword around and struck again, the force of the blow sending the man stumbling back, away from where Jacob lay on the road.

Stephen pressed toward him, his jaw set and eyes intent. Their swords struck, danced in a whirlwind of silver, then clashed again. The green-cloaked man was much bigger than Stephen, yet Stephen parried every blow, slicing, stabbing, and swinging with expertise, one moment springing from danger and the next darting forward to deliver a powerful attack. A thrill passed through Ellie. She'd never seen swordsmanship like it.

What more surprises do you have for us? she wondered.

"Ellie!" Alice's cry brought her back to the battle. She twisted to see a guard advancing on Alice and hurriedly loosed an arrow. It caught the top of his arm, sending him staggering back with a scream. Looking around wildly, Ellie saw that the rest of the guards were down, or locked in battle with the rest of the League. Stephen and the man in green were still dueling furiously.

Now's my chance!

She ran to the coach door. The lock was big and heavy, but she grabbed a rock from the road and slammed it into the wooden door until it splintered. The door fell open.

The interior of the coach was dark. Ellie jumped onto the step, blinking as her eyes adjusted. It was empty. There were no glittering jewels here, just two padded benches facing each other. Bitter disappointment bubbled inside her. The baron had been talking about the crown jewels, hadn't he? How had she gotten it so wrong?

Something stirred on the floor beneath one of the benches. Ellie crouched down to look.

Huddled beneath a cloak was a boy. He was young— about eight, she thought—and his eyes held the mute terror of an animal in a trap.

"Who are—"

But Alice was yelling another warning: "More guards coming! Ellie, we need your help!"

"Stay here out of danger," Ellie told the boy. He nodded.

She leaped from the carriage and slammed the door shut. A party of men on horseback were thundering up the road toward them. They came from the direction of the baron's castle and wore his colors—green and a sickly purple.

"I know them," Stephen said. His color was high and there was a smear of red over his cheekbone. "See that one on the far flank? He's deaf in his right ear. That short one's stronger than he looks. And him"—he pointed at a man who looked nearly as broad as his horse—"we need to deal with him first. He's the best fighter among them." He pulled off his scarf, which was knotted around his waist, and wound it around his face to make a mask. "Don't want my father to know where I am," he explained. "Not yet, anyway."

The broad man galloped toward the skirmish with his sword drawn. "Give us your cargo, in the name of Lord de Lays!" he roared.

Ralf shot Ellie a confused look. "If this new lot belong to the baron, who do the men guarding the carriage work for?"

There was no time to wonder further. The original guards—those who could still stand—scrambled to regain their weapons and their horses.

"We'll never surrender to you," the man in green spat,

limping toward his mount. His face was even bloodier than Stephen's.

The broad guard gave a yell of fury and his men broke into a charge.

"Out of the way!" yelled Ellie. "Move!"

The League scattered, Ralf and Alice hauling Jacob, who still looked dazed, clear. In the road where they'd been standing, the two groups of guards met in a clash of metal and a roar of curses. Ellie's knees went loose when one of the guards nearly decapitated a rider in the baron's colors, his sword swinging just shy of his opponent's ear. The man in green took on the baron's biggest soldier and was knocked from his horse for the trouble. The huge man swung around again and sent the green-cloaked man flying backward with a sword swung low into his stomach. He fell flat and lay still. Blood began to pool on the road around him.

The League seemed forgotten, both sides intent on finishing the other off. "Time to go," said Ellie, shoving them in the direction of the trees.

"But what about the jewels?" asked Alice.

"They're not here. Get away while you can—I'll meet you in the trees!"

"Meet us?" Ralf said. "Come *with* us!"

"Just go!" Ellie ordered. To her relief, they did. She

ran back onto the road, toward the coach. The rasp of swordplay and the gasps of wounded and dying men sounded all around her. She dodged blades and fists and swung the broken carriage door open once more.

The boy was standing now, watching the fight through one of the grilled windows. For a moment he startled, but when he saw it was Ellie, he breathed out with relief.

He's so little, she thought. If there were no jewels, then he must be the cargo the baron was trying to claim. Ellie would not leave him here to be kidnapped.

"Don't be scared," she said urgently. "I'm getting you out of here. Come on, take my hand."

He hesitated for a heartbeat, then slipped by her and jumped lightly to the ground. Ellie reached for him, but he wriggled from her grasp and began running, back up the Kirklees road in the direction his coach had come from.

"Please come back!" Ellie cried over the din of the battle. "We want to *help* you!"

The boy stopped.

"We're the League of Archers," she panted, running to meet him. "You know the Merry Men? We're like them."

At this the boy turned. When Ellie held out her hand, he grabbed it, and they ran together into the trees, to where the League were waiting.

7

"ANOTHER NEW MEMBER?" ALICE SNAPPED
when she saw Ellie running toward them with the boy.
The others were waiting under the spread of an oak tree,
far enough from the road that the sounds of battle faded
under the sigh and rustle of the forest.

"Shut up, Liss," said Ralf, elbowing his little sister.

"Is everyone okay?" Ellie asked urgently. "Any injuries
that need tending?"

Everyone showed off bruises and scrapes, but nothing
worse. Jacob looked pale, a bruise blossoming on his forehead from where he'd hit the road, and Ellie worried for a
moment he was more hurt than he was letting on. She was
taken aback when he turned to Stephen and held out a hand.

"Thank you," he said stiffly. "For helping me. For saving my life."

"Anytime," said Stephen coolly, but Ellie could see that he was pleased. He took Jacob's hand and shook it.

"You fought well," Margery told him. She looked sheepish. "I'm glad Ellie let you stay."

Stephen grinned widely. Under the oak tree his face was latticed with moving leaf shadows; dirt and blood were smeared on his cheek. Right now, Ellie noticed, he looked nothing like the arrogant boy in black she'd met at the castle—he looked like a true member of the League of Archers.

"I believe I owe you my thanks too."

It was the boy from the coach. He stood a few paces away from the League and gave them a formal little nod.

"Though I don't thank you for attacking my carriage," he added. His voice shook slightly, yet he carried the air of someone used to being taken notice of. His face was framed with close-cropped blond hair, his eyes brown and serious, his chin sharp. He wore a velvet tunic of midnight blue and red silk leggings. His boots were buffed to a gleaming shine. Compared with his attire, even Stephen's expensive clothes looked shabby.

"We didn't exactly mean to attack you," said Ellie. "We

didn't even know it was you in the carriage. We thought it was . . . well, treasure."

"The crown jewels, I bet." The boy's voice was getting steadier. "Everyone wants them, but nobody knows where they are."

Ellie was taken aback by this. "That's right," she said. "We were after the jewels. But I told you the truth when I said we're like the Merry Men. We don't want the jewels for ourselves—we want to use them to help people."

The boy looked at her doubtfully. "Help? That's what my father and all his friends say. But none of them really mean it."

"So who is your father, then?" Alice asked, her voice hard. Ellie threw her a look. "What's your name?" she asked in a kinder tone.

He hesitated for a moment. "Tom." Then he cleared his throat and straightened his spine. "Thomas Woodville of the House of York. My father is Lord Woodville. He's in London and I'm on my way to meet him there."

"But why would Lord de Lays want to kidnap you?" Ralf wondered.

The boy shrugged. "I expect he wanted to ransom me. My father's very rich. The baron has always been jealous of him."

"That sounds about right," Stephen said grimly.

A branch snapped nearby—probably just an animal passing through, but Ellie was taking no chances. It was high time they put some distance between themselves and the Kirklees road.

"Come on," she said to Tom. "We can't stay here any longer—the baron's guards are bound to come looking for us. Let's go to our camp. Then we'll find a way to get you safely to your father."

It suddenly felt terribly important to Ellie that they do just that. In different ways the entire League had lost their fathers. Ellie's had vanished to the Crusades. Margery's butcher father, and Jacob's fletcher one, were too integral to Kirklees village to leave it for the forest. And Master Attwood, father of Alice and Ralf, had been fading away since their mother died. He, too, still lived in the Kirklees village, but he was nothing like the man Ellie remembered from back when Mistress Attwood was alive. And of course, when it came to fathers, in many ways Stephen had drawn the worst lot of all. How to reunite Tom with Lord Woodville was at least a problem possible to solve.

She tried to take his hand once more, but Tom drew back.

"You saved my life, and for that I am grateful," he said stiffly. "But I can't leave. My . . . my uncle was hurt. I need to find him."

"It's too dangerous," said Ellie. "It'll be best if you just stay with us."

"I thank you, but no. And I'm sorry." He turned on his heel and ran into the trees.

"I suppose we're following him, then?" Alice grumbled.

"If you can keep up," Ellie shot back, and took off.

The boy was quick as a rabbit, with a surer step than she'd expected. As they got closer to the road, Ellie realized—with considerable relief—that she could no longer hear the din of battle. Ahead of her, Tom dashed out of the trees, then stopped short at the edge of the road. She nearly ran into his back, the League spilling out behind her.

The battle was over. Broken bodies, of horses and men, lay in the dirt. The quiet was eerie. Three saddled horses stood abandoned, one of them cropping the grass on the verge. Stephen grabbed its bridle. "We should keep the horses," he said, running a hand over its sweat-soaked nose. "Could be useful."

Tom looked wildly around, then ran to a body in the road. Ellie recognized its green cloak, now muddied and twisted—Stephen's dueling foe. A puddle of blood lay around him.

"No, Tom, it's too late," Ellie cried, but the boy was already on his knees, heaving the body onto its back.

The man gave a rasping groan. Everyone started with surprise.

"He's breathing!" Tom shouted. "He's alive!"

Ellie rushed to his side. The man's clothing was bloodiest on his front, so she pulled open his jerkin, revealing the wound—a deep gash in his stomach where, she now remembered, the baron's soldier had sunk his blade.

"How bad?" breathed Ralf.

Ellie closed the jerkin. "Bad. If he's to have any chance at all, he'll need stitches."

"You said you'd help me," Tom said shrilly. "You swore it. You said you were like the Merry Men, that you want to help everybody. So help him. Please . . ."

Ellie looked at Margery, who shook her head. She knew a bit of herb lore and didn't mind cleaning a wound, but stitches were beyond her. Maid Marian knew a fair amount of doctoring, but when anyone had been brought to the abbey hospital as badly injured as the man in green, there had been only one nun who could mend the wounds.

"Sister Joan," Ellie said. "If anyone can save him, it's her."

Tom sagged with relief. Now they just had to get his uncle to the abbey alive—and into the hospital without Mother Mary Ursula catching them.

The sun was setting over the abbey's crumbling stone walls. The fermented scent of late-season apples wafted over from the orchard, and the familiar, falling-water call of the nightingales rang from the eaves. At times Ellie had felt trapped inside the abbey, and she had certainly escaped it to hunt in the forest almost every night. But she'd felt safe there too. Under Marian's loving guidance the abbey had been her home. Now, with Mary Ursula as mother abbess, the walls of the abbey didn't so much look protective as resemble a prison.

Ellie, the League, and Tom were waiting for their chance to break in. Tom's uncle lay on the ground at their feet. They'd carried him here using his own green cloak as a stretcher, his wound packed with yarrow by Margery. She'd said the leaves would slow the bleeding, and had bound the wound shut as best she could with a strip of her tunic. The man groaned, but his eyes hadn't opened at all. He needed Sister Joan's skill, and fast.

A bell tolled. The sun lowered to an orange slice above the trees. Inside the abbey, Ellie knew, the sisters would be leaving their tasks and making their way to the chapel for compline, the day's final prayer. The way to the hospital wing would be empty.

"Let's go," she said.

It took all seven of them to get Tom's uncle over the wall without jostling him too much, and even so he groaned in pain as they set him on the grass on the other side. "Sorry," whispered Margery, adjusting his bandage. "Not far to go now."

It wasn't far at all, but their heavy burden made the stretch from the wall to the kitchen door seem like miles. They hurried toward it through the apple trees and lengthening shadows.

The door was unbolted. Ellie let them in, giving thanks for Sister Bethan's forgetfulness. Stephen, Tom, Margery, and Jacob carried the man, and Alice and Ralf flanked Ellie with their bows ready.

As Ellie expected, the kitchen was empty. The wooden table was swept clean; the dough for the next day's bread sat resting on the sideboard, draped in a cloth. Ralf ran his fingers over the barrels of grain lined up against the wall. "Is all this food?" he whispered, his eyes wide.

Ellie nodded. "Oats and barley," she remembered. She'd been surprised too when she first came to the abbey. Living in the village, she hadn't imagined so much food existing in the world. The rest of the League were staring about in wonder too, at the sacks of flour and metal flagons of milk. Ellie realized anew that although life in the abbey had hardly been perfect, in many ways she'd been far more fortunate than her friends.

Stephen alone seemed oblivious to the array of plenty. He was at the door, peering into the corridor beyond. "All clear," he whispered.

They carried the wounded man into a dark hallway, shuffling along until Ellie pointed them toward the passage leading to the hospital wing. The sounds of compline carried faintly toward them—the nuns' voices chorusing the prayers, snatches of hymns—but they met no one on their way. Ellie sent up her own prayer that their luck would hold.

She hurried ahead to open the heavy hospital door. The air in the stone-walled room was close, thick with the scent of dried herbs and illness. The walls were stained with smoke, lighter in the places where paintings and illuminated scriptures had once hung, before Marian, when she was mother abbess, sold them to raise funds for the villagers. Shutters were pulled close over the windows, and the only light came from a fire burning in the hearth, illuminating the twenty or so narrow wooden beds.

Ellie had worried that there wouldn't be a free bed for the wounded man. Now she saw that only four held patients, huddled under white sheets.

There should be far more than this, she thought. When Marian was the abbess, there had almost never been an empty bed. Life in Kirklees was hard, and cold winters, fevers, and long hours working on the farms took their toll. These empty beds didn't mean there were fewer sick and injured villagers, Ellie knew.

It's Mary Ursula, she thought furiously. *She's not taking them in.*

The few patients who were at the hospital lay still. In the dim light Ellie couldn't tell if they were sleeping or just watching quietly. She led the others toward one of the empty beds, and they eased Tom's uncle down as softly as they could. His face tightened and his eyes fluttered. "God save the king," he mumbled.

"He's no idea where he is," Ralf whispered, shaking his head.

Pain skittered over the man's face. "The king," he murmured again. His skin was terribly pale, his hair damp with sweat. "God save him."

"I need to find Sister Joan," Ellie whispered. "He can't go on like this much longer. You can find your way out, can't you? I'll meet you just over the wall."

As Stephen began leading the rest of the League away, a voice cried out from one of the beds. "Who's there?" It was a man with a bandage around the top of his head. He pushed himself up on his elbows. "Sister?"

His voice roused the other patients. In the bed nearest Ellie a woman sat up, a withered thing with hair like strands of hay. She clutched a hand to her throat. "Good Lord. It's the League of Archers!"

Ellie and her friends exchanged horrified looks.

"I recognize your faces from the 'Wanted' posters," the woman went on. "The baron's men have been nailing them all over the village. Bless you, I can't believe you're here!"

Ellie saw Ralf smile and Jacob stand a little straighter. "Please don't tell anyone," she said.

"After you rescued Maid Marian?" said another man, who had a straggly beard. "After the help you've given to Kirklees? Not for a pot of gold and the baron's head on a plate."

The woman reached out and clasped Ellie's fingers. "You're doing us proud, girl. It's like we've got Robin Hood back."

Ellie was too pleased to speak.

One by one the patients insisted on shaking the League's hands. After pressing the last frail palm, Ellie pointed toward Tom's uncle. "He's a friend of ours," she explained. "He's badly wounded. Help watch over him, will you?"

"A friend of the League is a friend of ours," the woman said.

"Thank you," said Ellie. She turned to the others. "We really must go."

Margery tucked the sheets around Tom's uncle, and they all hurried out into the dark passageway. *Now to find somewhere to wait for Sister Joan,* Ellie thought—and her heart leaped into her throat.

Sweeping toward them was a group of nuns—and in the center, her features sharp with candlelight, was Mother Mary Ursula.

8

"MERCIFUL FATHER!" CRIED A SHORT, ROUND nun named Sister Hilda. "It's the *outlaw!*"

Despite the panic pumping through her, Ellie had the urge to roll her eyes. Hilda was barely older than her, a newly ordained nun with a tendency to cry when she read her favorite psalms. She knew Ellie's name good and well.

Mother Mary Ursula thrust her candle before her. "You!" she gasped. "Elinor Dray! How dare you set foot in this holy place?"

Ellie stepped in front of the others. "Let us pass, Mother. We're not here to make trouble—we've only brought a patient to Sister Joan. We'll leave now, and we won't come back."

"You think I believe that?" Mary Ursula's laugh was high and edged with hysteria. "The days of this nunnery being run by outlaws and degenerates are done. I'm no Maid Marian—"

"No, you're not," Ellie said.

The abbess continued in a growl. "I'm no Maid Marian, thanks be to God. I don't care if you rot in a cell or if you hang, but you won't be setting foot in my abbey again. Sister Hilda!"

Sister Hilda's eyes went wide; she already looked a blink away from weeping.

"Send word to the baron's castle. Tell him I've got Elinor Dray and a pack of outlaws for him to arrest." Her eyes shone with glee. "Hurry!"

The younger nun bobbed a curtsy and took off at a run.

Ellie and the League began to follow in Hilda's wake, but another nun—Sister Matilda, who was as broad and strong as a blacksmith—moved to block their path.

"Will you fight nuns?" Mother Mary Ursula asked acidly. "I'd think that was too ungodly even for the League of Archers. Bar the doors!" Two of the sisters behind her rushed to do her bidding.

Ellie gave a snort of disgust. "Is it godly to hand us over to be hanged?"

Mother Mary Ursula slapped her, sending her head ringing. Alice yelped in outrage.

"Enough!" growled Stephen. Ralf tried to step protectively in front of Ellie.

Mary Ursula ignored them all. She shoved her face so close to Ellie's that Ellie could see the red veins that blotched the abbess's cheeks. "Marian always had too gentle a hand with you," she hissed.

"Maid Marian is ten times the woman you are, and every sister here knows it," Ellie shot back.

"I wonder if you'll remain so willful when you're in the baron's dungeons. Or at the end of the hangman's rope."

Ellie feinted back as if she were going to push Mary Ursula—as if she could really push a nun, even one as wicked as Mary Ursula—and when she flinched away, Ellie darted to her other side. Mary Ursula tried to grab Ellie, but she ran past.

"Rush them!" she called back, feeling a hot surge of triumph as the rest of the League came tumbling along behind her, the startled nuns left behind.

Her boots thundered on the flagstones of the passageway. It was like a bad dream, fleeing for her life through the place that had been a home to her. She felt like a deer, the hunt on its heels. "This way!" she yelled to the

League, spinning around a corner and across a wide hall-way, through a knot of startled nuns and toward the great front doors. She twisted the heavy metal handle: locked.

She gave a cry of frustration. Stephen rammed the doors with his shoulder, but it only made them rattle.

"My father and his men will be here soon," he said, brows drawn with worry. "There's got to be another way out."

"The garden door," said Ellie. "Follow me!"

The League sprinted after her as she took off toward a low door that led out to the orchard. A novice she didn't recognize startled out of their path, knocking into the gardening tools stacked beside the door.

"Ellie!"

It was Sister Joan, running up behind them. Her kind, round face was flushed with exertion. "The garden door's locked," she panted. "All of the doors are. Go to the hospital—the windows there are large enough to climb out of."

"Sister Joan!" cried another nun angrily. "Shame on you for aiding a criminal!"

"Do you see criminals here?" Sister Joan said starch-ily. "Because I don't! Shame on *you*, Muriel!"

Sister Muriel tried to throw herself into the League's path, casting her arms out to catch at them, but she was elderly and they sprinted past easily, tearing back to the hospital. But that door was shut now too.

"No!" cried Ellie, wrenching hopelessly at the handle. Alice beat her fist against the wood in despair.

"The kitchen," Ellie said.

They were fast running out of options. If Sister Bethan knew they were here—and surely by now she must—she would do everything possible to help them escape. Ellie led the League onward once more, past old Sister Muriel again, who shook a fist at them, down a passageway, and to the kitchen. The door was open.

Thank God and Mother Mary and all the saints, thought Ellie. The warm, familiar shape of Sister Bethan was inside, struggling to open the back door that led to the garden.

"Locked," she said shortly as the League tumbled into the room. Her face was full of rage. "One of the abbess's fools has taken the key."

"Mind your words, Sister." Mother Mary Ursula walked into the kitchen with her head held high, triumph written all over her face. "The baron's men must be close. I see the criminals have brought their bows—I suppose they'll be needing them now."

The sight of her triumphant, spiteful face made Ellie's blood boil. *I reckon I could shove a nun after all. . . .*

"God forgive me," she said to Sister Bethan—and

98   LEAGUE OF ARCHERS

pushed Mary Ursula so hard she fell backward onto a pile of flour sacks. Mary Ursula shrieked with rage.

Sister Bethan actually looked gleeful. "Run," she told them.

Run they did. But there were no more ways out to try. Ellie was instead looking for somewhere they could barricade themselves, to give them some chance of holding out against the baron's men. She could see the fear etched into her friends' faces, and felt it too, but she was determined to fight until the end.

She realized they were running through the nuns' chambers. The little bedrooms were empty—everyone in the abbey, it seemed, had rushed to hinder or help the League's escape—but something made her falter outside the largest room. It belonged, she knew, to Mother Mary Ursula, because it had been Marian's before. When she saw its contents, red rage ran through her: On the walls hung the few paintings the abbey still possessed, which used to be in the refectory. A seraph statue that had once stood in the chapel now presided over the new abbess's bed. In a corner was a glitter of riches Ellie couldn't quite make out in the dark. When Maid Marian slept there, the room had been spare and clean. Now it looked like the chambers of a greedy lord.

Ellie tested the door. "Not strong enough," she said,

imagining the baron's men snapping through it as easily as a hay bale. So on they went.

"Where now?" Ralf panted.

"The refectory," said Ellie.

"The refectory?" Margery looked confused. "Is there a way out there?"

"I wish," said Ellie as they tore down yet another passageway. "It's the farthest place from the front doors. It'll give us time to get ready to fight."

They rushed across a hallway, sending a group of nuns scattering.

"Maybe we won't have to fight," said Stephen, his voice heavy. "I'll talk to my father—I'll convince him to show mercy."

"Will he listen to you?"

Stephen shook his red hair from his eyes. "He has to. I'm his son."

But he didn't sound convinced. And given what they knew of Stephen's relationship with his father, Ellie wasn't either. As they ran to the refectory, her heart beat with a sickly rhythm. Lord de Lays would bring as many guards as he could muster, she could count on it. He wouldn't let Elinor Dray slip through his fingers again. The League's chances of getting out of this were slim, she knew. And if they didn't, she'd have let down all of them.

She and her friends would be facing the gallows, perhaps even Stephen, too.

Stop thinking like that, she told herself sharply. *It's not over yet.*

The refectory had a long wooden table where the nuns took their meals. At the far end was the pulpit, where Maid Marian had read the scripture while they ate, and behind that a window. By now darkness had fallen and moonlight shone through the stained glass, sending slivers of colored light over the large room. The image in the window depicted Saint Jude, a bearded man with hollow eyes, holding a crook. Ellie could almost have laughed.

Saint Jude, the patron saint of lost causes.

And maybe their cause wasn't lost after all. Saint Jude was offering them a way of escape.

She took off at a run toward the window.

"What are you doing?" Margery cried.

Ellie slammed her bow into the lowest panel of glass. It crazed through with cracks. With another blow the pane shattered, a rainbow of fragments tinkling to the floor.

"I'm getting us out!"

Her friends ran to her side, striking their own bows hard against the glass. In moments there was a gaping hole where Saint Jude had been. Stephen swaddled his fist in his cloak and knocked out the last jagged shards around the edges.

Footsteps rang in the doorway. Ellie turned to see Mother Mary Ursula rush in, sweaty strands of hair coming loose from her wimple. "Vandalism, too!" Her voice trembled with rage. "Does your depravity have no end?"

Ellie ignored her. "You first, Margery, you're the shortest," she said. "Hurry!"

Ellie and Ralf aimed their bows at the nuns as the League scrambled through the broken window one by one, thumping to the ground below. Neither of them would ever fire on a nun, but Mary Ursula didn't need to know that. It was clear she believed Ellie and her friends capable of anything.

When Stephen leaped through, Ellie told Ralf to go too. He hesitated for a moment, as if reluctant to leave her alone, then climbed through. Ellie lowered her bow so she could follow—and Mary Ursula instantly flew down the refectory toward her.

"You vile girl! You animal!" she shrieked. Ellie jumped up onto the window ledge as Mary Ursula's fingers grasped at her arm, the nails digging into her. Ellie had never seen anyone so angry before. "You won't escape justice," she spat. "You won't!"

"You don't know what justice even means," Ellie said

coldly. She wrenched free and dropped down into a crouch on the grass below. The rest of the League were waiting for her, their anxious faces peering through the darkness.

"Thank God we've made it out of there," said Alice fervently, pulling Ellie to her feet. "I never thought nuns could be so terrifying."

Ellie felt like they'd been trapped in the nunnery for days, but the position of the moon told her it had been an hour at most. Still, they could not afford to linger. She led them back through the orchard to the wall. All stealth forgotten, they sprinted like a pack of hounds. Over the wall they scrambled. Jacob boosted up Margery. Alice reached down to help up Ralf then Tom. When Ellie was about to vault to the other side, Stephen, crouched on top of the wall, caught her arm. He pointed toward the other side of the abbey. "We're just in time."

Silhouetted against the night sky was a band of soldiers, cantering toward the abbey doors. Even at this distance Ellie could catch the glint of armor and weapons. The baron's men, a force of at least thirty.

"Father will be furious," Stephen said.

They jumped down together. Ellie's heart was racing—from the chase through the abbey and the exhilaration of escape. But as she followed her friends into the forest, and the cool sanctuary of the trees closed around them once more, she knew that Stephen was right. The baron would be livid that Elinor Dray and her band of outlaws had escaped once more. What would he do in response?

9

IN THE CLEARING WHERE THE NEW FARM AND houses were being built, Jacob paced back and forth. He ran his hands through his sandy hair until it stuck out like dandelion fluff.

"How *dare* he?" he ranted. "How dare he take their *home*?"

Ellie could see there was no calming him—and she could hardly blame Jacob for being so upset. That morning they'd left the Greenwood Tree to come and help the villagers, and found Master and Mistress Galpin in the clearing. When Jacob had seen his parents, his face had opened into a grin, then gone fearful. Sure enough, the baron's men had evicted them from their house the day before.

And he did this before we escaped him at the nunnery, Ellie thought bleakly. *What will he do now that he's really angry with us?*

"They've lost everything because of him!" Jacob went on. He waved a hand at the tent the League had put up for the Galpins' first night in the forest—worlds away from their fine house. "They can't cope with this—my mum's used to sleeping in a proper bed. And cooking over a *hearth*. And—"

"Jacob," Ralf said sharply. "Yours isn't the first family he's done this to. And you've not lost *everything*—you've just lost your house." He glanced toward Ellie.

Jacob's hand flew to his mouth. "Oh, I'm sorry, Ellie," he said. "I didn't think. At least I've still got parents, haven't I?"

"It's all right," said Ellie. "I know it's hard. Let's help get them settled, shall we?"

At the edge of the clearing Master Galpin was grooming his horse, Juniper. The Galpins were the first horse-owning family to join their camp and would need a stable as well as a house. Mistress Galpin stood uncertainly beside the small heap of what belongings they'd managed to bring with them, sorting and resorting what she had. From a sack she pulled out a dress—a pretty one, with embroidery on the sleeves and lace at the collar.

Jacob smiled ruefully. "At least Mum brought her best pig-mucking dress. See, she's all ready to be a farmer."

Maid Marian, who sat nearby plucking a pigeon, laughed. "They'll get used to the outlaw life, Jacob. I promise. It's not an easy way to live, but it's better than the alternative. At least you'll see a lot more of each other now."

Stephen emerged from the woods, a stack of firewood in his arms. When Master Galpin saw him, he put down Juniper's brush. He stalked over to Stephen and leveled a shaking finger at him.

"You," he said, his voice icy. "I know you, Stephen de Lays. It's because of your family we're here!"

Jacob put a hand on his father's arm. "Father, please . . ."

He shook him off. "Your father took everything we had! First he poisoned my business. Next he drove away my son. Then he took the roof from over our heads!"

Stephen stood silently. His chin was lifted, his pale-blue eyes unreadable.

"Not even going to try to deny it?" spat Master Galpin. "What are you doing here, anyway?"

"Stop!" Jacob shouted. "It's not Stephen's fault, Father. And it's a good thing he is here. If he weren't, I'd be dead!"

Master Galpin turned from Stephen to his son. Mistress Galpin gasped, a hand flying to her mouth. "Dead?" she cried. "What do you mean?"

"He saved my life," Jacob said. "We were fighting and he stopped a man from killing me."

"He's on our side, you see," said Ellie. "He can't help who his father is."

The fight went out of Master Galpin. He looked like a doll that'd lost its stuffing. "If you saved my son, then I'm grateful to you." He touched an unsteady hand to his hair, as red-blond as Jacob's but thinner. "I'm sorry. I'm . . . not myself today."

Stephen gave him a nod. "None of us are. We're all victims of my father, aren't we?" His tone was conciliatory, but he held himself stiffly, head tilted back. Ellie wondered if Master Galpin's outburst had affected him more than he would let on. At least one thing had gotten easier: She clearly didn't have to worry anymore about Jacob losing his head and shooting Stephen with an arrow.

She looked around to say as much to Marian, but she was no longer there—she'd moved to one of the new tents, where she was kneeling beside a red-faced Tom Woodville. He was holding a hammer in his small hands and using it to drive tent pegs into the ground. His fine clothes were sweat-drenched, his cloak abandoned.

Marian put a hand to his forehead. "Some water is what you need, child," she said. "You're working yourself far too hard. Won't you stop and rest?"

"I thank you," said Tom in his oddly formal way. "But I'd rather be busy. I'd like some water, though."

LEAGUE OF ARCHERS

Marian went over to one of the barrels they'd set up to catch rainwater, and Ellie followed. "That boy wants to forget something," Marian murmured, dipping a tankard into the barrel to fill it. "He keeps his body busy to stop his mind from pondering."

Ellie looked over to where Tom was hammering again. His blond hair was stuck to his little head with sweat. He had a lot to want to forget—his father far away and unreachable, the baron on his tail, his uncle left to Sister Joan's care. The sooner he was reunited with his father, the happier he would be. "We need to get a message to Lord Woodville," she said.

"Lord Woodville?"

"Tom's father. He's waiting for him in London, it's all Tom's thinking about—well, that and his uncle, of course."

"Lord Woodville of York?"

"Yes," said Ellie. Then she caught the confusion on Marian's face. "What is it?"

Marian shook her head. "That can't be right. Lord Woodville has no children. There was a lot of gossip a year or so ago about his estate being left to the Crouchback family when he dies. Friar Tuck has his ear to the ground and heard it all."

Ellie stared at her. Was Marian mistaken? Or was Tom lying?

Before she could say more, Margery and Alice broke through the trees. The moment she saw Alice's face, Ellie was running to the tree stump where she'd propped her bow.

"The baron's men," she shouted. "They're following us!"

"What happened?"

"We were out hunting and they saw us," panted Margery, her face stricken with guilt. "We thought we'd shaken them before we headed back toward camp. But we were wrong."

"How many of them?" Ellie asked. "How close? Did you hear what they said?"

She felt Marian standing behind her. Jacob left his parents to join them; Master and Mistress Galpin were watching Margery and Alice with frank terror. Stephen strode over, his face tense.

"Three of them, but there'll be more," Alice said. "And they're nearby. They're searching the forest—they know, Ellie. Maybe they don't know what we're doing, but they know we're here. The baron will round everyone up, interrogate them. . . ."

Panic rippled through the clearing like flame through fabric. People dropped tools, snatched up children and belongings. An old woman started to cry.

"What can we do, Ellie—where can we hide them?" The anguish in Margery's voice gutted Ellie. She looked around at all they'd built. The shelters, the animal pens, the bakery. The heaps of potatoes, the smell of food and fire, the bunched herbs drying in the sun. Everything here meant life or death for these people. *So we've got to fight for it!*

"Ralf, Jacob, Alice, Margery—you stay here. Arm yourselves and arm anyone who can fight. Stephen, got your bow?" Stephen nodded, his face going hard and focused, the way it had when they were fighting Tom's uncle on the road. "Then go and get it. We'll hold them off as long as we can."

Ralf watched Stephen run to do what she'd said. "Why him?" he asked Ellie in a low voice. "Why take him and not one of us?"

"Because the villagers trust you—they'll follow your commands. I'm not sure they'll take orders from Stephen de Lays."

When Stephen had collected his bow and slid his sword through his belt, Ellie led him in the direction from which Margery and Alice had come. Behind her Ellie could hear the League giving orders: "Hide the young and the old in the shelters," Alice was yelling. "Everyone else, grab anything you can crack a head with and get ready to fight!"

Soon the clamor of the frightened villagers faded. Ellie and Stephen were moving away from the Greenwood

Tree, in the direction of the baron's castle. The leaves rippled green and orange and yellow overhead, and a layer of those that had already fallen crunched under Stephen's feet—he hadn't yet picked up the trick of walking soundlessly through the forest.

There came a yell in the distance and Ellie tugged on the back of Stephen's jerkin. "Hear them?" she whispered. "Go slowly now."

He shrugged her off. "I know what I'm doing. I've been in battle, remember."

The men's voices were closer now, and with them the sound of tramping feet. Ellie peered through the trees and thought she saw the flash of a cloak. "We don't have time to brag," she said. She pointed to a young oak. "Climb up. We might be able to catch them as they go under us." She hoped that by surprising the men from above, they could disarm them without killing them.

But it might come to killing, a tiny voice told her. *It might come down to choosing between letting them live and saving everyone at camp.*

She swallowed down her dilemma. Carefully she lifted herself into the lowest branches, Stephen climbing up behind her. From there she saw them—a group of soldiers, swords out, swinging them like farmers scything grain. The steady whoosh and grunt was broken off by a soldier's shout. A net shot up from the ground, closing around him like fingers making a fist. In an instant he was high up in the tree.

Ellie clapped her hands over her mouth, stifling a laugh. Jacob had set a few net traps around camp in the hopes of catching game; the soldier was their first quarry. He squirmed against the ropes, his arms grabbing at empty air. The men on the ground startled back, cursing, then laughed too.

"How's the view from up there, Richard?" one of them called.

The soldier responded with a stream of breathless profanity.

"Patience!" one of his friends responded. "You enjoy your rest. We'll cut you down once we've routed the outlaws . . . if we remember."

"You'll cut me down now, or you won't sleep another peaceful night in your lives," the soldier named Richard growled.

The rest of them laughed, one of the men already climbing the tree to rescue his comrade. When both were safely on the ground, they resumed their scything, disappearing into the trees.

"There's seven of them," Ellie whispered. "Alice said three."

"Soldiers have a way of multiplying," Stephen said. "There will be more coming."

"We can't let them get as far as the camp. We have to lure them away!"

"And how will we do that?"

"Maybe . . . maybe I can get behind them and shoot at them from there."

Stephen gave her a scornful look. "And get yourself killed? Not too clever. Luckily for you, I have a better idea." He swung his legs over the branch and dropped to the ground, landing in the tall grass below the tree.

"Stephen!" Ellie hissed. "What are you playing at?"

He put a finger to his lips, then ducked down into the undergrowth. Ellie growled with annoyance. If the men heard him, she'd have no choice but to fire at them. *Why can't he do as he's told for once?*

She started as, below, stone struck metal. In the bushes came a sudden flare of light.

Stephen stood grinning up at her. Nocked to his bow, poised to fly, was an arrow—and it was on fire.

10

"NO!" ELLIE'S VOICE WAS DANGEROUSLY LOUD. "Are you mad? We're standing in a forest!"

Stephen's blue eyes flashed. Then he shrugged, and before she could do anything else, he sent the arrow flying toward the soldiers.

Ellie dropped hard from the branches to the forest floor. "You fool," she spat at him.

The arrow arced through the branches, then disappeared from view. Alarmed cries went up from the baron's men. Ellie pushed past Stephen and took off toward the arrow.

"Ellie, stop! I'm warning you!"

She kept running. Another arrow arced high over her

head, a streak of fire. It landed with a storm of sparks. Then came another. The flames on the first went out, but the second one caught, the grass it was embedded in smoldering. A bush starred with white honeysuckle flowers whooshed up into flames.

What am I doing? she thought. Did she think she could stamp the burning arrows out? Would the baron's men shoot her before she got a chance to try?

By now she could see the soldiers again. A third arrow landed so close to them that they startled back. A clump of fallen leaves exploded into flames. Sparks shot up, catching the end of a branch. Fire danced along its leaves, and in a frighteningly short space of time the whole tree was on fire. Ellie gaped at it in horror.

She suddenly had a vision of the ancient Greenwood Tree crackling with flames. *No! I've got to stop this!*

Running toward the fire would do no good. She needed water—and help.

She turned and sprinted back toward Stephen, so filled with rage she could barely feel where her feet landed. He was nocking yet another burning arrow to his bow, his blue eyes dancing wildly as the flames reflected in them.

"Look, they're running away!" He laughed, pointing through the trees at the fleeing soldiers. "I was right, it worked!"

Ellie snatched the bow from his hand. The arrow fell. She stamped it out, her boots smoking, then slammed the bow against a trunk. It snapped in two, the pieces hanging limply from the string.

Stephen looked at her like she was mad. "What the—"

"The whole forest could burn down because of you!" Ellie screamed. She jabbed a finger to where the flames were spreading, already covering a distance the length of the abbey's garden. "You'll kill us all!"

She shoved past him and pelted back toward the camp. She ran like a rabbit with a fox on its heels, leaping over fallen logs, barely flinching when a branch whipped her cheek, ignoring the thin trickle of blood. She burst out of the trees and into the camp. The villagers, clutching their makeshift weapons, turned to stare in confusion as she charged across the clearing. "Ellie!" Alice called out. "What's happening? Are they close?"

"I sent them away!" It was Stephen, his voice ringing with victory. He must have followed her.

"We'll all be running away soon. There's a fire, and it's spreading!" Ellie reached the barrels of rainwater. "Everyone grab one of these and follow me!"

The villagers dropped their weapons and ran for the barrels. Children peeked from the windows of the shelters, gaping at the smoke that now curled above the trees.

A boy of five went running toward the flames; his mother followed fast behind, shrieking as she scooped him off his feet.

"I don't understand," said Ralf, heaving up one of the barrels. "How on earth did a fire start?"

"I'll tell you later." She shot a venomous look at Stephen. He looked genuinely bewildered by her reaction—which only made her angrier. She lifted a barrel and shoved it to his chest. "Go," she said icily, then turned back to grab her own.

The air filled with shouts as everyone worked together to fight back the blaze. The terror Ellie felt was as big and bright as the flames. When she was very small, she'd knocked a candle onto her parents' big bed. The flame had knifed neatly through the coverlet, the orange flames turning the white to black char. Her father had put it out before it spread too far, but she'd never forgotten the welling terror, the helplessness of watching the straw doll she'd been playing with turn to ash. She knew flames were hard and hungry; they didn't care about anything but their own appetite.

It was far worse now, in the open air, miles of vulnerable forest stretching around them. She ran back and forth again and again, directing the barrels toward the places where the fire was worst. The water did its work;

the damp ground helped with the rest. Finally she, Jacob, and Margery stamped out the last of it with their boots.

All around them was an island of wet black ruin—but beyond it, the vast green stretch of Sherwood Forest. *Safe.* She clasped her hands.

"Thank you, Saint Jude," she murmured. "Our cause isn't lost quite yet."

"Amen to that," said Marian, walking toward them. The hem of her dress was filthy with ash, and her silver hair fell loose around her cheeks. "How did this happen, Ellie? Did the soldiers try to burn us out?"

"Ask him." Ellie jerked her chin toward where Stephen sat on an upturned barrel.

"Yes, I started it. And I'd do it again," he said. "I got the baron's men to leave, didn't I?"

Ralf swore under his breath. Marian gave Stephen a strange look, blame mixed with pity. She put a hand on Ellie's scratched cheek. "Are you all right?"

Ellie nodded. She was too angry to say any more.

"We can't stay at the camp, Ellie. The baron's men will be back. Soon, I think."

The forest was still standing, but it was only a matter of time before the soldiers reported back and the baron had the area properly searched. And when they found the farm and the new houses, they would tear them down.

Everything they'd built would be lost. Ellie rubbed her eyes. The disappointment was unbearable.

"The villagers need somewhere safe to hide until this trouble blows over," said Marian.

Ellie nodded. She forced herself to put aside her own anger and frustration and instead focus on the problem at hand. The villagers needed to be protected, somewhere large enough and hidden enough to keep them safe from the baron's men. . . .

"I know the perfect place."

She strode back into the clearing, Marian, her friends, and Stephen following. All around her villagers milled about, speaking in low tones or clutching children to their chests. "Listen!" Ellie threw up her arms. A sea of anxious faces turned toward her. "We've worked hard to build this place. We thought we could stay here forever. But it isn't safe anymore—the baron's men have seen to that. Now we have to leave, and quickly, before they come back."

"Where are we supposed to go?" said a young mother, her voice edged with hysteria. "I've already left my village behind to take up with you in the woods. We're already sleeping in a half-built home, with barely enough food. Now what are we supposed to do?"

An uneasy murmur rose from the crowd. Ellie took a

deep breath. "We're going to the safest place in the whole of Sherwood Forest. The Greenwood Tree."

The villagers' restlessness shifted to excitement. "The Greenwood Tree!" a man said to his daughter. "That's where Robin Hood lived with his Merry Men."

Ellie caught eyes with Ralf, who stood next to Alice near the back of the crowd. His face was bright with surprise, but Alice's arms were crossed warily over her chest.

"Ralf," she called, "Alice, Jacob, and Margery. Each of you take a group of villagers with you. Lead them around the traps, and keep everyone as quiet as you can." She beckoned the nearest family to follow her. "Take anything you can carry, but not so much that you can't run," she told them. All around her the rest of the League were doing the same, Marian lending a hand too. Gripping her bow tightly, with a group of villagers at her back, Ellie set off for the Greenwood Tree.

By long practice the League fanned out, so the baron's men wouldn't be able to catch all of them at once. But before they'd gone far, Stephen caught up with Ellie.

"Didn't have enough blindfolds?" His voice was sour with sarcasm.

"What?"

"Well, I seem to remember you making me wear a blindfold when you took me to the Greenwood Tree.

You made a pretty big deal out of it. Now you're leading everyone right there?"

"What am I supposed to do?" she retorted, waving an arm at the straggle of villagers behind them, picking their way awkwardly through the trees. "How could I possibly lead twenty blindfolded people through Sherwood, let alone past the traps around the Greenwood Tree? Besides, it would take so long to blindfold them, your father would find us before we'd even finished tying the knots."

Stephen raised his eyebrows. "I'm surprised you're so sure. I just hope all this noise doesn't lead my father's men right to us. Still, as long as you think you're doing the right thing . . ."

"Of course I am."

But his words burned within Ellie's gut, as hot as one of the embers that had been smoldering on the forest floor. She'd made the right decision—hadn't she? *It's the only way to keep everyone safe,* she told herself. But the flames of unease wouldn't die down.

She guided the villagers past the pit trap with its rows of jagged spears, and around another of Jacob's nets that was suspended from a tree. Tom Woodville was with her group, his little face solemn as he clambered over a fallen log. With every step the villagers took, branches cracked and leaves rustled. Not one of them had learned to move like a wild thing through the trees, the way the League had. Ellie felt as ungainly as an animal with a broken leg. With the League, she moved swift and silent, and everybody kept up. With the villagers, she had to be aware not just of the traps but of fallen logs they might fall over, tendrils of deadly nightshade they might not recognize, divots in the ground where they might roll an ankle.

It's not their fault, she reminded herself, but she couldn't help calling back to them: "We need to move faster—as fast as you can go. But whatever you do, stay behind me!"

She ignored Stephen's smug look.

By the time they reached the Greenwood Tree, every creak and clatter sounded magnified in her ears. She led the villagers through the covering of greenery with relief. They gasped as they stepped into the clearing, staring up at the tree. A little girl, Ada Webb, fell to her knees and ran her hands over the grass. "It's real," she breathed.

Ralf arrived in the clearing at the head of his party. He ran to the tree's trunk and scaled it to the platform where they stored their extra weapons. He tossed down bows and clutches of arrows to the villagers waiting below and climbed back down with a clutch of knives stuck into his belt. Margery, Alice, and Jacob arrived with their groups. They distributed the remaining weapons, and everyone spread out around the edges of the clearing. Ellie nocked an arrow and aimed it into the rustling trees, waiting for the first appearance of a guard—the edge of a cloak, the crack of a step.

Her heart slammed and her throat rasped dryly as she swallowed. If anyone came—if anyone had followed them—they would have to leave the Greenwood Tree. Robin Hood's secret shelter would be lost to them forever, and they would have nowhere else to go.

She kept watching the trees, questions crowding her head. Was it by chance that the baron's men had spied Margery and Alice? Or were they out in the woods looking for them? *This could be his revenge for what happened at the nunnery,* she thought.

The minutes passed. Ellie could hear the villagers growing restless, some of them dropping their weapons and retreating to the clearing. Still she aimed into the woods as her shoulders grew stiff and her head ached from straining to hear the guards' approach.

"No one's coming," Stephen was saying loudly to a group of villagers. "Like I said, I scared those guards away. You should have seen them, they ran like rabbits! They won't be coming back after that."

"He's right," said Ralf, who was stationed next to Ellie. "Much as I hate to say it."

Slowly Ellie let her bow fall to her side. "The danger is passed!" she called out. "We can drop our weapons now."

Immediately the air in the clearing seemed to grow light. People were laughing, peering up into the Greenwood Tree's branches, climbing around its roots, and wondering at the platforms and pulleys high over their heads. A woman named Helen snatched up a tin cup from beside their campfire and raised it high.

"To Stephen—the boy who scared off the baron's soldiers with nothing but a few arrows!" she cried.

A cheer went up around the clearing. Jacob clapped Stephen on the back. "Our fights would end a lot faster if we always used flaming arrows," he said. "Or flaming swords!" Stephen laughed and gave Jacob a mock punch on the shoulder.

Master Galpin held out his hand to Stephen. "You fought back against your own father," he said seriously. "I had the wrong end of things when I met you. I hope you'll forgive me."

Stephen shook his hand enthusiastically—and the other hands thrust out toward him. The attention made him preen like a cat, his blue eyes bright, his movements full of swagger. He whispered something to Jacob, who erupted with laughter.

"*He's* changed his tune," said Ralf.

Ellie felt her jaw go as hard as stone. "Unbelievable. Why can't Jacob see through all that showing off?"

Ralf jogged her with his elbow. "Stephen's no leader, Ellie. That'll always be you."

Ellie felt herself flush with annoyance. "You think that's what I'm worried about? It's not that, it's the fire. Stephen could easily have burned down the forest. He could have killed us all."

"I know. Everything worked out in the end, though, didn't it?"

"Right. But what if the next time he does something stupid we're not so lucky?"

"Well, we'll just have to stick together and keep an eye on him, won't we?"

Ellie gave Ralf an affectionate nudge with her shoulder. *Thank the saints I've got you,* she thought.

They stood a moment longer, watching Stephen accept the gratitude of the villagers and the League. Even Alice looked impressed by what he'd done.

Am I being too hard on him? Ellie wondered. *Am I forgetting how far we have to go to keep ourselves safe?*

Maybe so. But she couldn't keep a dark thought from preying on her. What if letting Stephen join the League had been a mistake after all?

LEAGUE OF ARCHERS

11

ELLIE HAD GOTTEN USED TO WAKING UP TO the sound of the Greenwood Tree's branches sighing in the wind. The murmur of Ralf talking, the bright shout of Margery's laugh, the sound of metal on flint as Jacob made arrowheads. But since the villagers moved to the Greenwood Tree, things had changed. Now she woke up to the sounds of children—crying, playing, calling out to their parents for comfort or food. Men and women talking to one another, arguing, making plans. Cookware clanging, fires being set, branches crackling underfoot. She heard all the sounds of a village, but trapped within the confines of the Merry Men's hideaway.

Ellie, Margery, and Alice slept in the tiny shelter in the

Greenwood Tree's arms that used to belong to Robin and Marian. Ralf and Jacob each slept on their own platform, which they were transforming into proper shelters whenever they had a spare hour, and Stephen had claimed one of the tree's topmost perches for his quarters—to show off, Ellie suspected. He liked to sit up there, long legs stretched out as he watched the sun go down.

The villagers slept on the ground, in tents, under awnings made of woven branches, or simply spread out under the stars, whole families huddled under blankets and furs. There was no camp for them to go back to and nothing left to salvage. The League had gone to see what was left of their abandoned farm the morning after they'd run from the soldiers. The soldiers had returned, just as Marian had warned that they would, and the sight of what they'd done had filled Ellie with horror. The huts they'd lived in were reduced to splinters and mud. Bread and a rabbit carcass lay uneaten in the dirt. The garden plot was trampled, the pigpen torn down, and the chickens slaughtered and left to go rank in the sun. She knew things would have been infinitely worse if any villagers had been there during the raid.

And yet, although she was glad to have kept them safe, sharing the Greenwood Tree was harder than she'd expected. The feeling that it belonged only to the League of Archers, a secret place of safety where they could follow in the footsteps of the Merry Men, had been lost. Now the clearing thronged with people, day and night. Ellie often found herself touching the bark of the Greenwood Tree, hoping it could keep them all safe.

That night, a week after the camp had been destroyed, Ellie woke in darkness to a sound that sent her stumbling blearily down the trunk, bow already hooked over her shoulder. It was the whistle of one of the lookouts stationed around the forest. As Ellie leaped to the ground and seized a torch that rested by the fire, the lookout broke into the clearing. She was a woman named Catherine, a farmer's daughter who'd turned out to be an able fighter and builder. She was tall and lean, and had cropped her hair as close as a man's after a few days of living in the woods. Ellie picked her way toward her, past the half-waking villagers strewn about the grass.

"What is it? Is the baron back?"

Catherine shook her head. "It's the sisters. The sisters of Kirklees Abbey."

At first Ellie couldn't make sense of what she'd heard. "Nuns? In the woods?"

Catherine nodded. "On foot. They're carrying with them a wounded man."

Tom Woodville's uncle!

It had to be. Ellie realized that in all the upheaval she'd forgotten to question Tom further about his story, and whether Lord Woodville really was his father. Was the wounded man even his uncle?

Quickly she woke the rest of the League. Torches flickering in the darkness, they followed Catherine through the woods, into a small clearing dense with ivy. Four shrouded shapes seemed to hover, ghostlike, at the end of the clearing, then resolved themselves into four nuns— Sister Joan, Sister Mary Louise, a novice named Grace, and Sister Bethan. Ellie ran to throw her arms around the elderly woman's neck.

"By the saints, girl, do you mean to throttle me?" grumbled Sister Bethan. But she hugged Ellie back just as fiercely.

Tom's uncle lay on a stretcher on the ground. His face was pale as milk and unhealthily damp. Ellie had a sudden, stark vision of Robin Hood's face as it had appeared just before he died. She crossed herself quickly. "Will he live?"

Another figure darted through the trees. Ellie's heart leaped into her mouth. Jacob whirled around, bow taut. "Who goes there?"

It was Tom.

The boy rushed to kneel beside the stretcher and

grabbed his uncle's hand. "It's burning hot," he said fearfully.

He must have heard Ellie and Catherine talking, Ellie realized, and followed them. "This is Tom, the patient's nephew," she explained. Right now it didn't matter if this was true or not—it was clear how much the man meant to Tom. She wondered briefly if he could even be his father, but could see no likeness between the sick man's rugged face and Tom's sharp one.

"Is he dying?" Tom asked starkly.

Ellie glanced toward Sister Joan. The nun clasped her hands together. "I'm very sorry, child. I don't know how to save him."

Tom's eyes filled with tears.

"We'll . . . we'll do all we can to help his wound heal," Ellie said quickly. "Won't we?"

Sister Joan knelt down and adjusted the sheet draped over the man. Her hands shook and Ellie saw darkness in her eyes. "It's not his injury that troubles him," she said. "Someone gave him a dose of poison."

"What?" gasped Ellie. Flickering torchlight showed the shocked faces of the League.

Sister Joan rose to her feet. "I've done what I can to stop it from killing him, but I fear it's not enough."

"We can't protect him, Ellie," said Sister Mary Louise.

She looked like she might cry. "We've been taking turns to keep watch, but what if it isn't enough?"

"If he stays in the abbey any longer, he won't survive," said Sister Bethan bluntly. "Someone will make sure of it."

"But who?" wondered Alice.

"Mary Ursula," said Ellie immediately. "Who else?"

It seemed that wherever there was trouble, Mary Ursula was involved. Hot anger filled Ellie, and something else, too—guilt. She'd sworn to Tom the abbey would keep his uncle safe. She should have known that with Mary Ursula in charge, it was a promise she couldn't keep.

"But it doesn't make sense," said Ralf. "Why would Mary Ursula want to hurt someone she's never even met?"

Ellie turned to Tom, who was still clutching the man's hand. "Do you know why?"

He shook his head, mouth clamped shut.

I'm going to have to ask him for the truth after all. . . .

"Tom," she said as gently as she could, "who is this man to you?"

"I've already told you. He's my uncle."

Ellie went to crouch down beside him. "Look, Lord Woodville isn't your father, is he?"

Tom said nothing, but Ellie noticed him flinch. *So Marian was right on that score.*

"I don't care why you lied, Tom. We need to know the truth so we can help. Is this man truly your uncle? Is he your father, maybe? We just want to know why Mary Ursula would try to hurt him."

The blood rushed to Tom's cheeks. Gently he laid down the wounded man's hand and got to his feet. "I don't know what you're talking about," he said stiffly. He waved a hand at the stretcher. "Now move my uncle to the Greenwood Tree. Immediately."

Ellie and the League stared at him. Sister Bethan tutted in disapproval.

Tom seemed to recollect himself. "Forgive me," he said, sounding suddenly exhausted. "I'm worried he'll only get worse lying here."

Ellie, Alice, Margery, and Jacob each took a corner of the stretcher, and Tom and Ralf went ahead to push branches out of their path. The nuns filed behind them as they carried the man through the forest.

"What about the other patients?" Ellie asked. "Are they in danger too?"

"There are no other patients," said Sister Joan.

"They've been sent away," little Grace added.

"The hospital's been closed down," growled Sister Bethan. "On that woman's orders."

Ellie was stunned. "But how could she justify that?"

Sister Bethan looked like she could strangle a stag with her bare hands. "Because the abbey has no money, or so she says. It's truer than it's ever been, I suppose, with her in charge. She dines well every night while the village starves."

"I've seen her chambers," Ellie said, remembering. "They looked like they belonged in a castle."

"In truth," said Sister Bethan, "she's just another baron, wearing a sister's habit."

On they walked. The League did their best to hold the stretcher steady, but whenever one of them stumbled, the wounded man groaned. "The king, the king," he muttered over and over. "God save him."

Ellie heard the catching of breath and looked around to see Sister Joan dabbing at her eyes. Ellie had spent hours working with Joan in her hospital, learning how to brew simple tinctures, set a sprain, clean and dress a wound, stanch bleeding, watch for infection setting in. She'd not been a very good nurse herself, but Sister Joan was a true healer. The hospital was where she belonged.

"Sister Joan, I'm so sorry—"

The nun shook her head briskly. "There's nothing for it, dear. Just do the best you can for this man. I hope a lesson or two stuck."

"I remember rhubarb helps with beestings," Ellie said meekly, and Sister Joan gave her a watery smile.

When they reached the Greenwood Tree, dawn was starting to break. Marian, alerted by Ralf and Tom, came running toward them, her cheeks flushed and her skirts in her hands. "My sisters!" she cried. She and Bethan met in a hard embrace. Marian pulled away and hugged the other three nuns in turn, each lit up with happiness at seeing their former mother abbess once more. Sister Mary Louise burst into happy sobs.

"There, there," said Marian, wiping Mary Louise's cheeks. "I didn't believe I'd see any of you again. Oh, how I've missed you."

The camp was starting to stir. Ellie led the nuns to the fireside, while Friar Tuck picked up the wounded man in his brawny arms and laid him down on a pile of blankets hastily gathered by Ralf and Tom. Margery drew up a screen made of branches, from which she usually hung drying rabbit pelts, to shelter him. Tuck and Marian listened intently as the nuns repeated their story.

Marian shook her head sadly. "Mary Ursula's capacity for treachery exceeds my worst fears. Has she driven you out? Do you need to stay here with us?"

"Thank you, but no," said Bethan. "Tempting as it is, we can't leave the novices alone with that woman."

The others were in agreement. "Though I dread going back," sighed Joan. "I joined the sisterhood to do good works, not to watch an arrogant woman grow her store of finery day by day."

Marian looked thoughtfully around the clearing. Ellie could see an idea coming into shape behind her eyes. "If the abbess has closed your hospital," Marian said, "we'll just have to open a new one. Right here."

Ellie smiled at her kindness. Marian was everything an abbess should be.

"Perhaps you could come back someday and bring us your unused supplies, Sister Joan?" Marian asked. As she and the nuns began to make plans for how the hospital would work, Stephen, who'd been watching curiously, sidled up.

"What is it?" Ellie asked coldly.

"A hospital? Is she serious?" He gave a scornful laugh. *Who does he think he is?*

"Why not? It's the safest place in the forest."

Stephen waved a hand at the villagers, who were lighting fires, shaking out blankets, and starting their day. "Look around you, Ellie. This place is crowded enough already. Now you want to add a hospital, too?" He looked at a woman chasing after two grubby children, his lip curling in distaste. "I thought the League was about adventures and battles and doing brave deeds. Not a village full of peasants, hiding out in the woods."

A village full of peasants? Ellie gaped at him, hardly able to believe what she'd heard. She pulled him away from the fire. She didn't want the others to hear this.

"I didn't ask you to join the League," she said, her face growing hot. "You chose it, remember? And no, the League isn't about us having *adventures*." She drew the word out ridiculously. "It's for them. The people. It's whatever they need it to be."

"Fine words," said Stephen, "but be honest. Is this really what you want? To live crammed in a clearing with the sick and the dying?"

Ellie seized his arm again and yanked him so he could see the wounded man behind the screen. He'd twisted around, so his blankets were cast aside, showing the weeping bandage around his belly. It was stained dark red. The man's face was gray as ash, and he groaned terribly. "Look at him!" she said furiously.

Stephen looked. His mouth twisted.

"I suppose you would cast him out into the woods," she said. "Do you know who you remind me of? Your father."

Stephen had turned a deathly white. At first Ellie thought he was angered by her words. Then she realized how shallow his breathing had become.

"You'd better sit down," she said, and drew him to a

tree stump. Stephen sat down heavily, worrying at the black scarf he wore knotted about his throat. His red hair was stuck to his forehead. "I'll fetch you something to drink," Ellie said.

She headed toward a nearby water barrel, trying to untangle her thoughts. She'd seen nuns faint plenty of times at the hospital when faced with a particularly gruesome wound. She'd nearly done so herself. Most of the novices at Kirklees Abbey had gone to great lengths to get out of hospital duty with Sister Joan. Maybe Stephen couldn't handle blood either? She hoped that was the case—she'd certainly rather he object to the hospital out of squeamishness instead of cruelty. *So how on earth did he manage at the Crusades?* she wondered. *He must have seen worse injuries there.*

Ralf came over to join her as she filled a tankard. He nodded toward Stephen. "I saw what happened," he said. "He's a baron's son, don't forget. There's probably a lot he's not used to."

"Well, there's one thing he's going to have to get used to, and fast—helping other people."

"I want to get used to it too."

The voice was Tom's. Ellie turned to see him standing behind her and Ralf.

"I've not really helped other people before," he said.

His cheeks reddened. "But I'm a quick study. Will you show me how?"

He looked older than his years, his eyes weary and wide—and completely sincere. He'd lied about his family, but there were plenty of reasons people kept secrets—some of them very good ones. Her instincts told her she could trust him, as strongly as they told her to worry about Stephen.

"Of course we will," she said. "We could use your help."

After the nuns were breakfasted and rested, and had said their tearful good-byes to Marian, Ellie shouldered her bow and led them back through the forest, guiding them around the traps. Novice Grace and Sister Mary Louise looked fearful—and Sister Joan faintly disapproving—but Sister Bethan's eyes shone. "And the Merry Men made all of these themselves?" she asked, gazing up at a net trap.

"Mostly. Ralf and Alice did a lot of repairs."

"I used to dream of fighting back like Robin Hood," Sister Bethan confided. "Oh, don't look so scandalized, Mary Louise. We all fight back in our own way. His was just a bit more adventurous."

They reached the ivy-draped clearing where they'd met during the night. "We'll find our way from here," said

Sister Bethan. Ellie hugged them all good-bye, squeezing Bethan extra hard.

"If you ever need game," Ellie told her, "if you ever need help . . ."

Sister Bethan put her hands to Ellie's face. "I know. But you have enough to worry about. For now you keep what you shoot for the villagers. We'll get by on what we've got. Besides, Mother Mary Ursula could stand to eat a bit less."

Ellie smiled and watched the sisters' backs until they disappeared into the leaves. The forest seemed to become completely still. No breeze stirred the air. Crisp morning light slanted through the trees, and the only sound was of birdsong.

Perfect hunting weather!

And why not? She had her bow and arrows with her. Lord knew they needed the meat—stores at the Greenwood Tree were growing low. Last night her breath had made puffs of smoke on the air, and this morning the thinnest layer of frost tipped the grass blades before the sun melted it away. Winter would be here before long. They'd need as much game as they could get, especially now that the possibility of having a farm of their own seemed as hazy as a half-remembered dream.

She walked quietly through the trees, scanning the

ground with practiced eye for signs of quarry. She had hunted since she was old enough to carry a bow, and even before that had helped her mother lay traps for rabbits. She knew how to spot a trail of crumpled leaves, how to tell if droppings were fresh, and that a snapped bough meant something larger—hopefully a deer—had passed by, and how to tell from the color of the broken wood when it had done so. The thin sun warmed her face, and she found herself relishing the familiar feeling of being all by herself in the forest.

Between two trees was a pressed-down bed of grass. Ellie touched her palm to it—still warm. The animal that'd sat there would still be close by. She unhooked her bow from her shoulder and took an arrow from her quiver. Moving even more carefully now, she followed the trail of minutely disturbed stones and blades of grass. It was a rabbit, she decided, and from the size of the trail, a large one—big enough to feed four.

The stillness was broken by a snapping sound. Ellie started. It was a branch cracking, she knew, and came not from farther up the rabbit trail, but from some distance behind her.

A deer! It has to be!

She whirled around. Bow raised, she darted through the trees, hoping she was quick enough, caught a flurry of movement, let an arrow fly—and pulled up sharply when, spilling through the bushes, she saw her quarry.

Tom stood frozen, both hands up, her arrow quivering in the trunk just over his head. For a moment they just stared at each other.

Ellie exhaled hard. "First rule of hunting—you never surprise a hunter."

His face broke into a wary smile and his hands came down. "I understand. What's the second rule?"

She shook her head, pulling the arrow from the tree and returning it to her quiver. She felt shaken at what she'd almost done. "You'd better get back to camp, Tom. I'm trying to catch us some rabbit for dinner."

"I'm staying." Again his voice had that vein of steel running under it—that suggestion that he was used to being obeyed. "I meant what I said. I can't just sit around the Greenwood Tree, eating your food and using your supplies, and sleeping under your stars."

She startled at the turn of phrase. Whoever's son he was, Tom was clearly well educated. "I don't mind sharing the stars."

"Let me do more," he said. "Let me play my part. Please?"

Ellie hesitated. The last person she'd taught to hunt had been Alice, and she hadn't been an easy student—she had a tendency to lose her temper when she felt she wasn't catching on fast enough. But Tom had a calmness to him, a watchful alertness that might make him a good student.

"Okay," she found herself saying. "I'll show you a few things."

For the rest of the morning they wandered all over Sherwood. She took Tom to a stream, where they saw ducks paddling and tracks in the soft earth. She pointed out the places a deer might like to feed, and a raggedy tree trunk where a buck had rubbed the velvet from his antlers. They ran hollering through the undergrowth, flushing a flock of pheasants into the sky. She brought down one, then another, enjoying Tom's look of awe.

"Here, you want to try? Hold the bow here and here, and always shoot just ahead of your target. See?"

She knelt behind Tom to sight over his shoulder, and knew his third arrow would hit just before it did.

"I got it! I got it!" He looked properly happy for the first time since she'd met him. "I've never shot at anything but a target before!"

"You said you were a quick study. You were right."

They gathered the arrows and the fallen pheasants and trekked on. Tom wanted to try for a rabbit, but the undergrowth was quiet, and Ellie still held out hope for a deer—pheasants and rabbits weren't going to feed everyone waiting for them back at camp. They ate blackberries off the bush, so late in the season they were at the edge of rot, with a high, syrupy sweetness that made Ellie's teeth sing. The shadows grew long, then the sun disappeared behind the treetops.

"Still no deer," said Tom morosely.

"There's one last place we can try."

An hour after the sun had dropped out of sight, they were crouched in the shadows beyond a crumbling stone hut. In the clearing that surrounded it, a doe and a stag dropped their elegant heads toward the ground, pulling up mouthfuls of grass.

"That's the gamekeeper's lodge," Ellie whispered.

"The *baron's* gamekeeper?"

"Shhh. Yes. He seeds the ground with clover to draw the deer. See?"

Tom nodded, but he looked unsure.

"Now watch what I do. This is different from shooting pheasants. Feel how the breeze is blowing toward your face?"

"I . . . suppose."

"We're standing on this side of the wind because you can't let the deer smell you. If they do . . ."

But the stag must have smelled something: It raised

its long neck and froze, its body tight with concentrated motion. Any moment it would bound into the trees and take the doe along with it. Ellie knew she had to be fast. She nocked an arrow, raised the bow to her shoulder, and trained it on the stag.

"Thieves!"

The harsh shout made her jump and her arrow fly wild.

The gamekeeper. Lying in wait, in the shadows of the house. Tom sucked in a gasp. Ellie shoved him behind her and brought another arrow to her bow.

The man strode out of his hiding place. He wore a tattered cape of brown leather over a woolen tunic and mud-encrusted boots. His hair was lank and greasy. "You stole my venison! Come out of there, you, let me see your face!"

"It wasn't us!" Ellie called.

"Was," the man growled. "You nicked it right out of my storeroom!"

Who would do something so stupid? Ellie cursed the thief inwardly. Now the gamekeeper would be watching his deer like a hawk hunting for mice.

Except, right now, his gaze didn't look that steady. He stumbled toward Ellie and Tom, his footsteps shambling. *He's drunk!*

"Let's run for it," she told Tom.

They turned to flee—and the gamekeeper whistled. "After them, Hotspur!" he yelled. And with a ferocious howl a dog launched itself out of the darkness.

It was black furred, with a dripping muzzle and powerful shoulders. Ellie and Tom sprinted back into the trees, but the dog caught their scent in a moment. Ellie turned to fire at it, but her arrow sped uselessly into the dark.

"Good boy, Hotspur!" came the gamekeeper's gleeful yell. "Bring them down!"

The animal tore through the ground cover and leaped up, its heavy paws slamming into Ellie's back. She crashed to the earth. The dog growled and snapped, its breath like rotten meat. One of Ellie's arms was pinned under her, and with the other she hit at the dog's head, trying to push its snarling jaws and yellow teeth away from her throat.

As she struggled, she glimpsed Tom, mouth open in horror.

"Run," she told him in a strangled gasp. "Go!"

He ran—but stopped after a few paces and bent to pick something up.

What by all the saints is he doing? she thought, screwing her head down into the dirt as the dog snapped at her. *There's no point in us both getting killed.*

When she twisted around again, Tom was right beside

her. He was holding her hunting bag of pheasants—she must have dropped it when she fell. "Here, dog!" Tom yelled. "Catch!"

He flung the bag. It went arcing through the trees. The dog snorted, wetly snuffled the air—and leaped off Ellie. It bounded past Tom, crumpling him to the ground, then disappeared into the trees.

Sweet relief flooded Ellie. She crawled over to where Tom lay. "That was brilliant," she told him, taking his arm to pull him up. But he drew it back with a cry of pain, his features twisted. His arm looked oddly limp.

"Hotspur?" came the gamekeeper's shout. He was getting closer. "Did you catch them, boy?"

"Sorry, Tom, but we've got to go." Ellie heaved him up with his other arm, and he gave a yelp that made her wince. She took his good hand and pulled him away through the trees.

It was harder to run holding hands, so Ellie kept their path as straight as she could. They passed the sounds of the dog tearing into its meal of pheasants. The yells of the gamekeeper faded away, yet Ellie didn't dare stop yet. Tom's breathing became more and more ragged as they ran, but he made no word of complaint. He let Ellie drag him through prickling underbrush and across a stream— she made sure they both got fully soaked, in case Hotspur remembered its duty and tried to catch their scent—until finally they reached a point about twenty minutes' walk from the Greenwood Tree.

"Let's rest," she panted, letting Tom go at last. Tom dropped to his knees. His face was taut, his fingers wrapped around his injured arm.

"Let me see."

Ellie gingerly peeled the sleeve back to his shoulder. The skin was unbroken but starting to purple and swell.

Tom sucked in air hard through his nose. "Sorry," he said through whitening lips. "I was too slow, he almost caught us—"

"Don't say that," Ellie said. "You saved me. I don't know what I'd have done if you weren't there. Made a nice meal for that dog, I suppose."

He laughed, then winced.

"I think the bone is broken," Ellie said. "Marian will be able to set it for you. You'll be okay."

Tom nodded bravely. "The Greenwood Tree really will be a hospital then. Me and my—my uncle, side by side."

They trekked back to camp, Ellie keeping their journey slow and steady for Tom's sake. They arrived to see a new tent raised, in the spot by the fire where Tom's uncle had been. *So there's our new hospital,* thought Ellie. She lifted the flap and ushered Tom inside.

Marian was cooking a poultice over a low flame, the sleeves of her dress rolled up. She dropped the pan when she saw Tom's arm, twice the size it should be and tinged the color of blackberries. Ellie hung back as Marian tested it with deft fingers.

"It's broken, dear—but it's a clean break. You'll soon be swinging swords and stringing arrows with the best of them."

Tom nodded, but his face was white now. The flight through the forest and the pain of his arm seemed to have caught up with him. He slumped into a seat beside the bed where his uncle lay.

"Hold out your arm," Marian said gently, and began binding a splint of wood to the swollen skin.

Ellie left them to it. She wondered what the rest of the League had been up to in her absence, and was drawn by a burst of raucous laughter on the other side of the Greenwood Tree. Following it, she found most of the camp gathered around Stephen, clearly well recovered from whatever malady had struck him earlier. He stood on a stump, a large bag slung over his shoulders. From it he pulled piece after piece of venison, handing out the purple chunks of meat to the villagers. He looked like a priest giving Communion to a devoted congregation.

An old lady put her piece of venison into her apron

pocket and grabbed his hand between both her own. "Such a good boy you are," she said. "Not a thing like your father!"

"It's nothing really," said Stephen, though he visibly seemed to swell. "I just wish I could do more." His bag empty, he tossed it to Jacob, who stood on the ground beside him. Jacob whirled it over his head, and both he and Stephen burst out laughing at some private joke.

Ellie had seen enough. "Hey!" she yelled, pushing through the crowd toward the boys.

Stephen looked around, surprised. He gave her his widest—and, he clearly thought, most charming—grin. He was infuriating. But the worst thing was she *had* once thought him charming, hadn't she? She could admit that to herself now. From the moment she met Stephen, she'd been dazzled by his handsome blue eyes, fine clothes, and haughty attitude. He was nothing like the village boys she knew. Now she saw him for what he was—an arrogant idiot. She felt thoroughly ashamed of herself for being taken in.

She snatched the empty bag. "You stole that venison, Stephen!"

"Who, me?" He gaped his mouth open in a mockery of shock, getting a snicker from Jacob.

"Yes, you! Right out from under the gamekeeper's nose, and I paid the price for it! Thanks to you, we'll never catch another of his deer again. He'll be guarding them like that horrible dog of his guards a bone!"

Stephen tilted his head back and looked down at her. He'd never seemed more like his father. "Look around you, archer girl." He held out an arm to indicate the entire Greenwood Tree. "Everything here is stolen. We're living well, we have everything we need, but don't forget that every bit of it was taken from someone else."

"That's not the point! By stealing that venison, you've cut off our supply. And winter will—"

"If everyone here played their part," Stephen said loudly, speaking over Ellie like she hadn't said anything at all, "we would have plenty." The watching villagers murmured in agreement. Ellie looked to Jacob, but he didn't say anything.

Stephen stepped closer to Ellie, speaking so softly only she could hear. "If we didn't waste our resources on people who can't help themselves, we'd never even have to hunt. We could just *take* what we want. We could have a life of adventure, not one of drudgery. Isn't that what the League of Archers should be about?"

Ellie's jaw dropped. She was so appalled that her tongue seemed to stick in her mouth.

"I'm right, aren't I?" murmured Stephen. He gave her another of his infuriating smiles.

"You know nothing about why we started the League," she told him coldly. "It was to carry on the work of the Merry Men—to steal from the rich, yes, but so we could give to the poor. *That's* what the League of Archers is about."

Stephen just gave her a pitying look.

Despairing of ever getting through to him, Ellie appealed to Jacob. "He's made things worse for us today. Can't you see that?"

Jacob glanced from Ellie to Stephen. The villagers who still lingered did the same. "Honestly, I can't see what he's done wrong. My parents will eat well tonight because of him. Everyone here will." He gave a shrug. "What's so bad about that?"

Stephen was watching him like a proud tutor. "After all," he said sleekly to Ellie, "it's not as if you've brought anything back, is it?" He turned on his heel, Jacob trailing after him.

Ellie felt like she'd been run through with a dagger of ice.

I wish I'd never met him, she thought bitterly. *I should never have accepted his help, or made that stupid promise. It would have been better for the League if I'd been captured.*

Even though she was surrounded by people, Ellie felt utterly alone.

12

JACOB'S SIDING WITH STEPHEN STUNG ELLIE badly. There had been disagreements among the League of Archers before, but nothing like this—and for the sake of the villagers, the League needed to pull together more than ever. Everyone was safe at the Greenwood Tree for now, but tempers in the clearing were running high. Families grappled for space by the campfires and in the shelter of the tree's roots. They fought over handfuls of berries. The ground was hardening with cold, making the task of building shelters difficult. Ellie knew that they needed to do something drastic if they were to keep everyone warm and fed—and that meant reviving the dream of the farm.

So they needed money, and she thought she knew how to get it. When she'd assembled the League to tell them her plan, Stephen had looked infuriatingly pleased with himself. "I knew you'd see sense in the end," he'd told her. "We can steal whatever we want. What do you want us to do?"

But even his support made her annoyed now, and she'd been avoiding him as much as she could.

Tonight they were putting Ellie's plan into action, and hiding outside the constable's house. She'd met the man before, on the day he and the baron came to the abbey to arrest her and Maid Marian. The house was a smart building of stone, one of the few in the Kirklees area—the peasants lived in simple wooden dwellings. It was hung with lanterns and set like a jewel in a circle of ornamental flower beds. The League were crouched outside the garden's elaborate metal gates.

The exterior told of the riches they were certain to find within: money; jewels, no doubt; valuables the constable had bought or stolen from his prisoners. Ellie had never forgotten his expression of amused disdain as he watched her and Marian being dragged off by the baron's men, or the way he'd held a knife to her throat. No, she wouldn't feel guilty about robbing this man. The house was like an egg, ready to crack open so they could enjoy the treasure inside.

"See that window on the second story, the one all covered over with ivy?" Stephen spoke in just over a whisper. "That leads to a corridor, not a bedchamber. If we climb in there at this time of night, there'll be nobody to see us."

"How do you know *that*?" Ralf asked.

"Because he's visited the house with his father, of course," Jacob interjected. "The constable never could've guessed he'd be back to rob it!"

Ellie rolled her eyes. Since the argument over the venison, Jacob had followed Stephen around like a gosling trailing a goose, hanging on his every word.

"Fine," she grunted. The knowledge was useful, even if she wished it had come from a different source.

They climbed over the gate and crept single file through the garden, Ellie at the lead. She ducked low, keeping to the hedge of neatly clipped box that framed the flower beds. The air was rich with end-of-season decay, the flowers shriveled into mulch. She made for the base of the ivy. In the lantern light she could see four or five thick trunks, each as wide as her arm, coiling together up the wall of the house. She pulled at the ivy to test it, and it took a few hard yanks to come off in her hand.

"Use it for balance, but keep your feet on the stone," she whispered.

She reached for a ridge in the stonework and hoisted herself up, feeling for footholds and handholds, and grabbing the ivy only when she needed to. She heard the rustle of leaves as the League came up behind. When she reached the window, she took an arrow from her quiver to lever open its wooden shutters.

Ellie slipped inside, stepping onto a polished wooden floor. Stephen was right—it was a corridor, and empty. A candle on a table was spitting wax and was almost burned out. By its light she could make out the frames of a row of doorways.

Stephen climbed in next, then tied his scarf around his face—should they be seen, he clearly didn't want his identity revealed. The others followed. Once all six of them were inside, the hall felt suddenly too tight. How could they possibly pass through the house unnoticed?

Think of the farm, Ellie told herself. *It'll be worth it.*

"This way," breathed Stephen. He led them down the narrow passageway. Silver candlesticks winked at Ellie from a small table, and she slid them carefully into the bag tied at her waist. A tiny painting in a gilded frame hung between two torches. Ralf lifted Alice up so she could take it.

Stephen jabbed his finger at a staircase that snaked down into darkness. "The constable's office is that way," he whispered. He'd told them about this earlier—the room he'd glimpsed during a visit with his father, which he'd described as being stuffed with treasures.

He began tiptoeing down the stairs, the rest of the League following. Ellie lingered, intending to bring up the rear. Her bow and quiver hung heavy on her shoulder. She prayed she wouldn't have cause to use them.

A door swung open. Ellie's heart leaped into her mouth.

A tiny figure in a white nightgown stepped out into the corridor. It was a little girl of about six. She rubbed her eyes with one hand—then saw Ellie standing at the top of the stairs. Her eyes went wide.

"Wait," Ellie whispered frantically. "We won't hurt you. Please don't—"

The girl screamed. In the silent house it was as loud as the great bell at Kirklees Abbey.

Goose bumps broke out all over Ellie's skin. She ran down the stairs, slamming into Ralf. He and the others were frozen with horror.

"What do we do?" he asked, panic in his eyes.

Ellie shoved him roughly forward. "Go, go, go!" she half whispered, half yelled. "Grab whatever you can on the way, but get out!"

Silence no longer a priority, they tumbled down the

stairs. Stephen was at the bottom. He stared at Ellie in disbelief. "Why are we running?" he demanded. "We've got knives and bows. They've got dressing gowns."

From the rooms above came the creaking of floorboards, the murmur of voices. The household was waking up.

"We haven't come here to fight," Ellie spat. "We're leaving. Right now."

Margery had already run to the front door, unbolted it, and flung it open. The night was a square of darkness, beckoning to them. Alice grabbed a vase and a candlestick and pelted toward it.

"You really think that'll be enough to pay for your farm?" said Stephen. "We came here for treasure, and we're not leaving without it. Come on, Jacob. Let's find the office."

Footsteps thundered on the stairs. They all whirled around to see an elderly man charge down them, his feet bare and his tunic streaming out behind him.

"Get out, thieves!" he bellowed.

Ellie strung an arrow to her bow but hesitated in an agony of uncertainty over where to put her shot that wouldn't harm him—at such close range, she couldn't be sure of not killing him—and suddenly the man was gripping her arm.

There was a hard, sickening thump. The old man's eyes went empty and he slumped to the ground. Stephen stood behind him holding a stone jug, his expression triumphant.

"What are you doing?" Ellie screamed. "You might've killed him!"

A woman gasped from the top of the stairs. "What have you done? Murder! Murder!"

Stephen glared at Ellie. "Hold back the next one with your bow, then. We're here to do one thing, and we're going to finish it. Don't you want that farm of yours?"

The man moaned at her feet. *At least he's not dead.*

A plump man wrapped in a tunic, a candle clutched in his hand, pushed past the woman and ran down the stairs. Ellie recognized his round face, purple with outrage—the constable.

"Get off my property, vagrants! If you've killed my servant, I'll have each of you strung up by your noses!"

Stephen leveled an arrow at his face. The constable breathed in sharply.

"Raise your hands," Stephen said from behind his scarf. The smile in his voice made Ellie feel sick. Overhead the little girl was sobbing. The woman on the stairs pressed the sleeve of her nightgown to her mouth, stifling a scream.

"Please," the constable said, putting his trembling hands in the air. "Please don't hurt my family."

All of it—the smoky torches and the girl's cries overhead, the constable and his terrified wife, the fallen man and Stephen's dancing eyes—swirled together in a terrible nightmare.

And it was all her fault. She'd brought Stephen into the League, she'd made the plan to come here tonight. She'd broken into a family's home and frightened them from their beds. Margery's eyes were wide and scared. Alice's expression was unreadable, like she'd frozen to stone. And when Ellie looked at Ralf's face, she was certain it mirrored what was on her own: dread and horror.

She wanted to scream. Was this what the League of Archers had become?

13

"STEPHEN," ELLIE SAID. SHE GRABBED HIS ARM, but he shook her off like she was little more than a gnat buzzing around the campfire. "Stephen, we're going. Right now."

But his eyes were far away, bright with that same wild glint that had made him send flaming arrows through Sherwood Forest. "Not until we've got what we came for. Constable?"

"What do you want from us?" It was the constable's wife, gripping the banister. Her face was streaked with tears, her mouth set with hatred.

"Your wife is smarter than you, Constable," said Stephen. "Tell her we'll be leaving with the best of your valuables, all those fine things you have decorating your office."

"Fine," the constable grunted. "Eloise, fetch George and Margaret. Tell them to load up a bag."

"A cart," Stephen said.

The constable hesitated. "All right. A cart."

"I'm particularly interested in that cloak you wear with the jeweled clasp. You remember the one? I'll know if anything's missing. And if it is"—Stephen pulled his bowstring tauter—"you'll pay the price."

The constable nodded miserably.

Margery moved to Ellie's side. "What should we do?" she whispered. "Stephen isn't going to leave, is he?"

Ellie shook her head. "Not without his spoils. We'll have to stay and make sure he doesn't hurt anyone."

Because suddenly Stephen was the only person in the room she was afraid of.

She was beginning to understand what little she knew of him. All he had told them of himself was that he hated his father and hated being sent to the Crusades. Hatred seemed to run through his veins, deep and dark. *And dangerous.*

The constable's wife darted into an adjoining room. Through the walls they could hear the house coming alive. Someone must have gone to comfort the little girl, because her sobs quieted. Wheels crunched from the garden—the cart being drawn up. Servants moved around them, carrying glinting treasures outside, shooting looks of fear mingled with disgust at the League. Ellie had been an outlaw for many months now, and a poacher for years before that. But this was the first time she had felt like a true criminal.

The constable, his hands still in the air, was peering at Stephen. "I know you, don't I?"

Behind his mask Stephen said nothing.

"I'm certain I recognize your face. Won't you lower your scarf and introduce yourself?" The constable's eyes narrowed. "Or are you too cowardly for that?"

"Shut up," Stephen said sharply.

The constable pursed his lips. A nervous-looking servant shuffled up to him. "The cart is ready, sir."

"Walk forward," Stephen said harshly.

The constable did as he was told. Stephen followed, pressing the tip of his arrow into the man's back. "Jacob, you cover me. Ellie and the rest of you, go ahead of us and make sure the cart's loaded. Watch out for that cloak!"

With no choice but to do what Stephen said, Ellie led the League outside. The peace of the gardens had been broken with shivering servants, one of them holding the head of a docile chestnut horse hitched to a laden cart.

It was piled with a king's ransom of treasures, so many riches Ellie's throat went dry. She saw the cloak with its glittering clasp laid out over the top.

"We're ready!" she yelled, hating the quaver in her voice, hating that she was following Stephen's instructions.

The constable came stiffly out of the house, Stephen behind. Jacob followed, holding Stephen's sword. Stephen kept his bow trained on the constable as he made for the cart, his aim not breaking as he climbed onto the seat at the reins. The rest of the League clambered up beside him. Ellie was about to follow but changed her mind.

She turned back to the constable. Her cheeks were burning with shame.

"This isn't what I wanted," she told him. He stared at her like she was raving. "I mean, this isn't what the League of Archers does—"

"I know who you are, Elinor Dray." His face wrinkled with disgust. "You fancy yourself another Robin Hood, don't you? I hated the man, it's no secret. But at least he had a code. Even thieves can have honor, they say, and I'll tell you one thing: Robin Hood never broke into anyone's *home*." His voice rose into an angry shout. "And he never terrorized anyone's family. You're no Robin Hood, and your gang are no Merry Men."

His words were like a volley of arrows. Each one of them struck home.

"Enough," growled Stephen. "Ellie, get in the cart, now!"

She climbed aboard, her legs shaking so badly she could hardly keep her balance.

She'd barely sat down, crammed next to Ralf, when Stephen set the horse to a canter. In moments they were clear of the gardens, through the gate, and thundering toward Sherwood Forest.

Ellie gripped the edge of the cart, knuckles white. They bumped through the forest, the horse tossing its head as Stephen pulled the reins this way and that. Ellie's stomach churned. She wanted to throw up, and not from the motion of the cart.

"Stop," she gasped.

"Not yet," said Stephen. "Let's get farther in. Then we can figure out a way to get all this stuff through the trees."

Bile rose in Ellie's throat. "Stop the cart now."

Ralf glanced at her and looked stricken at whatever he saw in her face. "Do as she says, Stephen!"

He yanked the reins. The cart ground to a halt, the treasures jangling. Ellie leaped down and stumbled to a beech tree, resting her head against the cool bark. She took deep breaths, gulping in the gentle forest air. After a long moment the nausea passed. She stood up straight.

"Ellie?" Ralf put a hand on her shoulder.

"Are you feeling better?" Margery called from the cart.

Ellie shook her head. "I feel terrible. I've never felt so bad in my life! What we just did makes me sick with shame."

"What are you talking about?" demanded Stephen. He hopped into the back of the cart and grabbed an enormous silver candelabrum. "Look at what we got tonight. We're rich!"

"And I'd rather we'd left without a single coin than acted like thugs to get it," Ellie flashed back.

"We're not thugs." To Ellie's shock, the words came from Alice, perched on the back of the cart. "The constable is the thug," Alice went on. "And so's the baron." She picked up a pair of silk gloves from the pile and gazed at them as if they'd spellbound her. "We've been stuck under the boot heel of thugs all our lives, and now we've finally got a chance to fight back." She dropped the gloves and stared Ellie in the eye. "What's wrong with taking back what we're owed? I'm glad about what we did tonight. It's no more than the constable deserved."

Ellie had never heard Alice string so many words together in her life. She looked like a fox caught in a trap, wild and unpredictable.

Ralf went over to his sister. "But, Liss . . ." She pushed away the arm he tried to put around her.

"I'm glad about tonight too," Jacob said baldly.

"We know *you* are," Ellie replied.

"What's that supposed to mean?"

"You agree with everything Stephen says now, don't you?"

Jacob's temper rose hot and fast. "You're the one who brought him to the League, Ellie! You're the one who wanted us to accept him. And the minute me and Stephen become friends, you get jealous and you can't stand it!"

"I'm not jealous!" Ellie snapped.

"I think you are," said Alice. "Just a little bit."

Ellie gave a sharp, hard laugh of disbelief. "Are you blind? Can't you see what the League has become since Stephen arrived?"

"It's become an efficient force," said Stephen coolly. "We got enough loot to eat all winter, to buy new weapons for anyone who wants them, and to start building your farm. Isn't that what you want?"

Ellie was too angry to speak. Margery linked her arm through Ellie's, and Ellie squeezed it gratefully.

"Ellie's right," Margery said. "I hate to think of the nightmares that little girl is going to have. And the constable's wife—she's not going to forget seeing an arrow pointed at her husband."

Ralf threw up his hands in exasperation. "Can we just stop arguing, please? We've got to get back to camp before the constable organizes a search party. Let's talk about it when we get there."

They made the rest of the ride in silence. Stephen drove the cart until the trees became too thick, then they used their cloaks to make bundles so they could carry the treasures the rest of the way. Ralf unhitched the horse and led it by the reins. They finally reached the Greenwood Tree as the sky started its shift from gray to blue and the first birds woke up to greet the sun. People were building the morning's fires and crawling sleepily out of their tents or down from the tree. When they saw the glittering bundles, their murmurs turned to shouts of amazement. The League heaped the treasures in a pile. As the villagers gathered to exclaim over them, Stephen stood by proudly. Ellie noted with disgust that he now wore the stolen cloak around his shoulders. It was a deep blue velvet, the clasp heavy with jewels.

"Just a few things we liberated from the constable," Stephen explained jauntily. He held out a necklace to Ellie. "Why don't you enjoy it for a moment? You have to admit, a little force is worth it sometimes. And it's not like anybody really got hurt."

Rage broke in Ellie once more, like a river bursting its banks. "You left a man lying on the ground with a cracked skull! You held an arrow on a man in his own hall! You would've hurt *children* if it meant getting your precious rubies and cloaks, I know you would've!"

He looked taken aback, but only for a moment. "And you wanted us to run away like rabbits!" His face contorted into a sneer. "Some leader you are!"

"I never should've let you join the League," Ellie snapped. "It's been nothing but a disaster."

Jacob barged toward her, his face flushed under his sandy hair. "A disaster? Was it a disaster when Stephen stopped the baron's men from finding the camp? Or when he fed us all fresh venison? Or is it a disaster that we've stolen enough from the constable to do whatever we want?" He looked as angry as Ellie felt. "A fat lot of good you've done for us lately. Where are the purses you swore to steal from Nottingham Castle? Or the crown jewels you were so sure we could get?"

Margery moved between them, her hands up like she was interrupting a sparring match. "Stop fighting! This is horrible!"

"Be quiet, Margery," Alice said with venom. "We didn't do anything wrong and you know it. Ellie just thinks she's high and mighty because she's got Robin's bow, and because *she* got to live at the abbey."

"Alice Attwood, you shut your mouth!" Ralf yelled.

"Got to live at the abbey?" Ellie repeated furiously. "I lived at the abbey because my mother was killed! The baron hanged her!"

"He killed our mother too," Alice threw back. "Or as good as. She'd have survived the sickness if we'd had enough to eat. You're not nearly as special as you think, Ellie!"

Ellie stared at her friend, barely recognizing her. Ralf caught her arm, like he thought she might launch herself at his little sister, but she felt too horrified to do anything. "We're on the same side, Alice," she whispered.

Alice's face softened, just slightly. "Without Stephen we'd be getting by on ducks and a couple of candlesticks. He's right. Maybe a bit of force is worth it. And maybe you're just too soft."

"Come off it, Alice," said Ralf. "We were helping people long before Stephen came along. And we did it without hurting innocent people. Like Robin Hood did."

Stephen laughed darkly. "That's the real problem here, isn't it? You're all so obsessed with following Robin Hood that you can't see what's obvious. If you want to fight back, fight back with everything you've got. And if you want to take what's yours, take it with both hands." His eyes flashed with icy fire. "And the funny thing is, Hood wasn't the saint you all pretend he was. I could tell you stories about him that would make you sick."

"You think we don't know that?" Ellie shouted. They'd learned the hard way that he was more than a legend—he had been a man, flaws and all. "He tried to be perfect, that's what counts. And when he failed, it drove him mad. He would never in a million years have terrorized little girls!"

"Stop," Margery cried. Tears were streaming down her face. "Stop it, all of you!"

Ellie snapped back to herself. For the first time she was aware of the crowd that surrounded them. She felt the weight of the villagers' eyes following her, the thick silence of dozens of held breaths. She couldn't see Marian, thank God, but Friar Tuck watched her from the back of the crowd, his face stony and his arms folded over his chest. *What must he think of us? What must they all think?*

"Margery's right," Jacob said into the silence. "We shouldn't fight. It's a waste of time." He dropped his head and spoke his next words to the ground. "Maybe the League should split up."

The words hung on the air like a terrible black cloud.

Margery began to cry again. Ralf looked like he might cry too. Alice, like Jacob, was looking at the ground. Ellie put a hand to her mouth, utterly crushed.

Stephen broke the silence. He strode up to the crowd, his jeweled cloak gleaming. "I want to fight back against my father and his wickedness with everything I've got!" he roared. "I want to make the nobles fear us as much as we've feared them! I want to take what we deserve and make them pay for all the years they've eaten off golden plates while you, the people of England, have starved! No matter what it takes, I swear I will never stop fighting back. Now, who's with me?"

Ellie thought that with his hands on his hips, and his head tilted back proudly, he didn't look like an outlaw at all, but the very baron he wanted to defeat.

Jacob went to stand next to him. Then Alice, carefully avoiding Ellie's eye.

"Liss!" Ralf cried, his voice cracking. She flinched at the sound of her brother's voice but didn't look back.

The villagers broke into murmurs, looking between Stephen on one side and Ellie on the other. Margery and Ralf pressed close against her, and she felt like she'd drop if they moved away.

A trickle of villagers began walking toward Stephen. First a few, then more. Jacob's parents were followed by Catherine and the rest of the lookouts. Next went most of the unmarried village men and some of the families. Tuck watched them go, his eyes sorrowful. A woman whom Ellie had once spent an afternoon teaching to wield a sword looked at her apologetically. "I stand more of a chance of being fed with them," she muttered, before bobbing a half curtsy and crossing the clearing. The crowd thinned until Ellie could finally see Marian, standing close beside Friar Tuck. She looked ashen. They came to stand next to Ellie.

The vast majority stood with Stephen. As well as Marian and Tuck, on Ellie's side were Ralf, Margery, and a handful of villagers—Elspeth, whose husband had left for the Crusades not long after Ellie's father; an elderly couple and their adult son; a knot of others. Tom Woodville was with her too, his broken arm now in a sling.

Ellie met Stephen's eyes across the clearing. "We're not leaving the Greenwood Tree."

He smirked at her. "You can keep your little tree house. I know a place on my father's grounds where we'll be safe."

If Jacob and Alice registered any dismay at being taken to the baron's land, Ellie couldn't see it. Stephen led his followers to the trees, pointing them toward a path through the forest. He himself mounted the horse that had belonged to the constable. He shook his jeweled cloak back, looking down at Ellie.

"You can keep your name, too," he said. "We're not the League of Archers anymore. Just call us"—he grinned widely—"the Merry Men."

14

THE CLEARING AROUND THE GREENWOOD
Tree held a new kind of quiet. Before, back when the
League first discovered it, the clearing had been filled
with the peace of birds and trees, and running water just
out of sight. Now it rang emptily with the quiet of having been left behind. Tuck was sharpening the cooking
knives on a whetstone; Marian was dealing with a horse's
cracked hoof. On one of the platforms high in the tree
Margery was hammering repairs. But all Ellie could hear
was Alice's and Jacob's absent voices.

It was even worse for Ralf. He'd barely spoken a word
since Alice left. At every crackle of the fire or rustle
in the trees, his head shot up, as if he was expecting to

see his sister stepping into camp. And every time she didn't, his eyes went a little duller. Ellie's heart ached whenever she looked at him. She couldn't have borne losing Ralf, her best friend and the closest thing she had to a brother. But to see how lost he was without his sister was hard to stomach.

Their hunt today was long and almost fruitless. Ellie tried to talk to Ralf about growing their own clover patch closer to the Greenwood Tree, to draw deer without the help of the gamekeeper. He just shrugged, then shot early and wide of their target, a brace of pheasants that had burst from their hiding place by the stream. In the end they straggled back to camp near dusk, each carrying a pair of scrawny rabbits. The clean scent of gathering frost clung to the air. A few of the villagers who'd stayed with Ellie were gathered on logs around the fire, huddled against the chill. Out of habit Ellie glanced around for Jacob and Alice, before remembering—for what felt like the thousandth time, each equally painful—that they weren't there.

Margery dropped down from the tree, dusting her palms together and looking skeptically at their bounty.

"Well . . . we can add a couple of potatoes to the pot to make it stretch," she said. Her voice was bright, but Ellie could tell she was only trying to be cheerful. "Tom dug some up this morning. Took him an age with just one good arm. He'll be pleased we're using them."

"It's not quite venison, is it?" said Donald, the man who'd stayed behind with his elderly parents. Ellie tried to like him, but he reminded her too much of Sister Jeanne, a Kirklees nun who could find fault with a cloudless sky. "I wonder how the others are eating," Donald continued dreamily. "The Merry Men. Maybe the baron's sharing with them from his table—they are with his son, after all. . . ."

"I wouldn't take a mouthful Lord de Lays offered me," Ellie said through gritted teeth. "And his son is near as much an outlaw as I am. I doubt the baron would give him a crumb."

Donald's mother sucked her teeth, pinching one of the rabbit's skinny legs. "Perhaps the new king will bring easier times for us," she said, as if to herself. "Things certainly couldn't be worse."

"If there even *is* a new king," Donald said morosely. "We haven't heard a word about it, have we?"

He was right. They had heard plenty about the landlord of the Stag and Stoat's new young mistress, Ellie reflected, but not a word about the new king of England.

"How *would* we hear about it, out here in the woods?" Ralf said irritably. He'd had little patience for anyone since Alice left. "And what do you care? Are you expecting to be invited to the coronation?"

Donald shrugged. "Things like that have a way of being known. Of course, I never got word of King John's death, either. The one who told me about it was *her*." He looked at Ellie with narrowed eyes, folding his arms over his chest. "And she's the same one who told us we'd be well fed."

A vision of the king's purpling face flashed before Ellie's eyes—she could hear again the terrible sounds he'd made before slumping over the banqueting table. . . .

"Hold your tongue," Tom told Donald. He'd come around from the other side of the clearing, his good hand drawn into a fist. "Ellie is no liar. King John is dead, and soon a new king will take his place. You can be sure of it!"

"And what would you know about such things?" sneered Donald.

Tom went red. Ellie put a hand on his shoulder. "It's okay," she murmured. "Let them complain. An argument with supper is as good as salt." It was something her mother used to say when her father wouldn't stop ranting about the barons, the taxes, the cruel truth that the villagers always paid the highest price for the king's decisions. She was right, too—he had always seemed to sleep easier after he'd had his say.

She turned to her friends. "It's true, though. Four measly rabbits isn't enough to fill everyone's bellies. We should go back out."

Margery nodded. "I'll come with you." She piled the rabbits in Donald's arms. "Here," she said tartly. "You start skinning. Friar Tuck will get you a knife."

Ellie tried not to think of Jacob as she, Ralf, and Margery went to the tent where they stocked the arrows he'd made, neatly topped with feathers, their shafts as true as any made by Master Galpin at his fletcher's shop.

Ellie pulled back the flap. The boxes of arrows were empty.

What was I expecting? As if the new "Merry Men" would have left them behind. She felt embarrassed to have thought otherwise—then angry. Jacob might have made those arrows, but Ralf and Margery had cut down the branches he'd used for the shafts. Ellie had shot the birds that had once worn those feathers. She kicked at the nearest tent peg, then kicked it again and again, until it jogged loose of the ground and sent the tent half toppling.

"Ellie, *stop*," said Ralf, cutting through her rage. "We'll make more. We'll manage."

Ellie turned to snap at him, but the words died in her throat. He was hurting as badly as she was. Worse. She

wanted to believe this was all Stephen's doing, but she
kept remembering the way Jacob had looked as he ran to
join his new leader: proud and excited, like he was setting off on an adventure. The way he used to look when
the League went hunting, back when they didn't have
anyone to feed but their own families and the abbey.
Alice had looked stern, a little sad, but certain of what
she was doing. That was almost worse—she had so lost
faith in Ellie, she didn't even think twice about leaving
the League of Archers behind. About leaving her *brother*
behind.

While Ralf and Margery set about gathering supplies
to make new arrows, Ellie went to find Marian in the
hospital tent. She was hovering over Tom's uncle, lifting
his head to spoon broth into his mouth.

"He hasn't woken," she said. "But his color is better—
see?" She looked around at Ellie, her eyes gentle. "You're
tired."

Ellie nodded, suddenly too sad to speak. She could
feel the corners of her mouth turning down and had to
put all her focus into not letting herself cry. *If just one tear
gets out,* she thought, *they all will.*

Marian led Ellie to the edge of the clearing, away from
the circle around the campfire. "After everything that
happened, you *should* be tired," she said, taking Ellie's

hands in hers. Her voice was low and soothing. "You should be angry and sad. You can mourn your friends leaving you, Ellie. You mustn't be ashamed of that."

"I . . . I never should've let Stephen stay!" The words came out on a rush of tears. And Ellie let herself cry.

She hadn't truly cried when Robin died, or when the baron took Maid Marian away. She hadn't cried when she believed they had no hope of saving Marian from the baron's dungeons, or when she learned about the horrible crimes of Will Scarlet. But now, with her friends far away and Ralf walking around like a bird with a broken wing, she sobbed as if she'd never stop. It made her feel eight years old again, lying in her novice's bedchamber, longing for her mother. Her shoulders shook as she hunched over, hugging her rib cage. She felt Marian's arms go around her and relaxed against her chest.

At last the hurt lightened, still there but bearable. "Oh, Marian, how could they have left like that? To follow *him* . . . And the Merry Men? Who is he kidding? It's an insult. To Robin, to Tuck, to you . . ."

"I've had worse said about me." Marian tucked back a piece of Ellie's hair.

"The League's my whole life," Ellie said. "It's everything to me, just like the Merry Men were for Robin. It's all I know how to do—and I really think it's what I'm *meant* to do. I've always wanted to be like Robin, I try to live up to his memory. And I know the Merry Men left him in the end. But he was an old man when that happened. How have I lost the League so soon?" She wiped her eyes. "I must be nothing like him at all."

Marian gave her a shake. "But you *are* like him. I should know, shouldn't I? I knew him best in all the world. You have his passion for justice, his inability to back away from a fight. His blind faith in the ones you love." Marian smiled ruefully. "But you have strengths Robin never had. You're not cocky, like he was. You don't fight just the biggest battles, you fight the small ones too. Robin could steal the throne right out from under a king but forget to shoot enough meat for breakfast."

Ellie smiled at this. She remembered how she'd met Robin, both of them trying to shoot the same duck—how competitive he'd been, how eager to show off his archery skills.

"You have the heart and mind of a leader, Ellie," Marian continued. "You are Robin's true heir. Not Stephen. *You.* Your friends will come back to you. They will. And you just have to open your heart enough to forgive them when they do."

By the time she stopped speaking, tears were running down her cheeks too. For a moment Ellie just held on to her hands. Wanting so much to believe Marian's words, but fearing the hope they gave her.

"I hope you're right," she said finally. "I pray that you're right."

Ellie yawned widely. She'd been up half the night with Friar Tuck, who'd taught her, Ralf, and Margery to make arrows by firelight. She'd spent the other half of the night planning. Hunting was scarce, and anything they planted now would freeze in the ground. If they were to feed themselves and their small band of villagers, they would have to do something bold.

They were following Marian through the woods; Ralf and Margery were as bleary eyed as Ellie. Only Marian looked alert, her eyes bright. In the early green gloom between trees, leaf shadows on her face, Ellie could see how she must've looked years ago, when she walked with Robin by her side.

The air had the held-breath quiet of early morning, the sun filtering weakly through the treetops. Their footsteps made ghostly shapes in the cold grass. The trees thinned, and Marian stopped by a wooden post. It was covered in lichen, but Ellie could make out a florid letter *C* carved into it. Two crossed swords were carved underneath.

"This marks the start of Lord Clerebold's lands," Marian said. "Good luck and good hunting!"

They thanked Marian and, as she turned back toward the Greenwood Tree, pressed on through the forest. Around the campfire in the early hours of that morning they'd at last struck upon a plan to feed everyone. They wouldn't wait any longer to buy what they needed to start their farm—they would steal it. Cows for milk to get them through the cold months, then to slaughter when the forest no longer had the grass to feed them. Chickens for eggs, a pig if they were lucky.

Probably even Stephen would approve, Ellie thought.

The trees became more scarce. Soon they were looking out over a big stone house with shuttered windows. Between them and the house rolled green fields dotted with cows, each looking far better fed than anyone living at the Greenwood Tree. Lord Clerebold was clearly rich with plenty to spare—and, as Ellie had told everyone last night, he was a friend of Lord de Lays's. Lord Clerebold was the man the baron had been plotting with at the banquet. Ellie had no compunctions whatsoever about stealing from him.

"Well? What are we waiting for?" Ralf said. He launched himself over the wooden fence that circled the property. Ellie and Margery followed. They kept their heads low and followed the edge of the field to where the largest group of cows was gathered. A couple raised their heads to eye the arrivals, but most carried on calmly cropping the grass.

"Me and Ralf will round up the cows," said Ellie. "Margery, you try to find a gate out to the forest. And if you can't find one, make one."

Margery patted the ax that hung from her belt. Nobody wanted to spend time learning whether you could coax a cow to climb over a fence.

"Should we split up?" Ralf asked Ellie. "I can go look for—"

An arrow thudded into the ground at his feet. He gave a yelp of alarm. Quick as a hawk, Ellie drew an arrow from her quiver, slotted it to her bow, and trained it over the fields. Margery did the same.

Ralf bent down and pulled up the arrow. "Look."

From its head to its fletching Ellie would know it anywhere: It was an arrow made in the style of Master Galpin.

Jacob.

He stepped out from behind a hay bale on the other side of the field—then froze, his face turning from suspicious to shocked.

"What are you doing here?" Ellie's voice sounded funny in her own ears.

Jacob shook his head. "I didn't know it was you. I wouldn't have—"

The front door of the stone house opened. A man with a scarf over his face strolled out.

Not a man—a boy . . .

Stephen pulled down the scarf when he saw Ellie. He strode to join Jacob and grinned.

"What did we do to deserve a visit from the League of Archers? Trying to steal Lord Clerebold's livestock, are you?" He shook his head mockingly, then tossed a full purse into the air. It jangled when he caught it. "Unlucky for you, this house is under the Merry Men's protection."

Ellie gaped at him. "Protection? Robin would weep! You're nothing but a gang of rich men's guard dogs."

"And you're too high and mighty to take easy money." Stephen hung the purse from his belt. "Go on back to your tree house, archer girl."

Ellie turned to Jacob in dismay. "And you're okay with this, are you?"

"Lord Clerebold's paying us well." Jacob kept his eyes to the ground, as if he couldn't look any of them in the face.

"You know this isn't right, Jacob Galpin," Ralf spat. "You know what you've turned into? You're the people we fight against. You're the people helping the rich stay rich and the poor get poorer!"

"I'm feeding myself and my parents!" Jacob burst out. "That's more than you can say. You're here to steal from Lord Clerebold, and I'm here to protect him. What's wrong with that? Besides, who cares what Robin would think? He's dead, and I'm not even in the League of Archers anymore."

"No, you're not," Ellie said. "You're on the side that shoots hungry people out poaching."

"We're hungry too, Ellie!"

"Jacob, you don't have to listen to this," Stephen said. He walked toward Ellie almost lazily and put an arrow to his bow. "By the order of Lord Clerebold, master of these lands, I order you to retreat. On pain of death."

Margery scoffed. "You wouldn't kill us. You don't have the guts. One day soon you'll be just like your father, lazy and soft and hiding in your castle. I think you were just like him all along."

Stephen's pale-blue eyes flashed and his fingers tightened on the bow. "Don't push me," he said, his voice tight.

Ellie turned to go. "You ought to be ashamed," she said to Jacob over her shoulder. "You're a disgrace to the memory of the Merry Men."

As they marched back toward Sherwood Forest, all the peace had gone out of the morning, all the hope had been squeezed from her heart.

15

"WELL, WORD IS FINALLY OUT," SAID FRIAR
Tuck. He sat heavily by the fire, his monk's robe cascading in folds of brown fabric around him. "They've found themselves a new king."

That night they were almost eating well—rabbit much plumper than the usual scrawny ones they found, the last of the season's blackberries, and loaves of bread Tuck had bought in Kirklees village. He'd clearly gone there in search of gossip as well as food.

Tom paused, midbite on his rabbit leg. "A new king?" he echoed.

Tuck took a swig of ale from his tankard—he'd been brewing beer in the Greenwood clearing—and swallowed a burp. "Aye, lad. Queen Isabella's traveling to Gloucester to see her son crowned."

Isabella, Ellie knew, was John's widow, and she vaguely remembered hearing that they'd had a son. He'd been born when her own mother was still alive; together they'd gone to listen to the church bells being rung to welcome the royal birth. She pictured what the young prince might look like now, a smaller version of his round, greedy father, stuffing himself with custard tarts while his country starved.

"Already?" Tom was asking. "Already they're crowning the king? Isn't it . . . it's too close to King John's death, isn't it?"

"Not close enough, more like," Tuck said knowledgeably. "You know what they say—'The king is dead, long live the king.' Might as well stick a crown on the prince's head and make it official."

Donald noisily sucked rabbit grease from his fingers. Supper was so good it had even given them a respite from his complaining. "Never liked a king myself," he said, "but it don't do to be without one for long."

"Only good king we've had was Richard the Lionheart," agreed Tuck. "But he was too busy at the Crusades to do much for England."

"But what about the new king?" pressed Tom. He'd set

aside his bowl and was eyeing Tuck seriously. "What does he look like?"

Tuck shrugged. "Haven't seen the boy myself, I'm afraid. I heard the news from Edwin Cripps in the Stag and Stoat last night, after he got too far into his cups. . . . Well, that's another story." He took another gulp of ale. "Young Edwin is scribe to the bishop of Worcester—and the bishop is the one who'll be anointing the new king, Henry."

"Anointing?" Ralf asked, his brow wrinkling.

Tom brought his fingers to his own forehead. "Like this," he said. "He'll touch the king's head with holy oil before he's crowned."

Donald eyed Tom doubtfully. "How do you know that?" he asked between chews.

"Unlike you, Donald, the boy has brains," Tuck said with a throaty laugh.

But Tom's words had struck Ellie, too. "How can they have a coronation without the crown jewels?"

"Edwin says they'll be making do with Queen Isabella's gold circlet," said Tuck. "It's the crown she wears. Well, they're not exactly making do—Edwin says it's made of three bands of gold wound together. More than fit for a king."

More than fit to pay for a farm!

Ellie raised her eyebrows at Tuck. He put down his

tankard and grinned. "Word is that the gold circlet leaves Nottingham tomorrow," he said. "For those who are wondering."

The following morning Ellie and what remained of the League were up before dawn. To intercept Queen Isabella's crown, they'd need to ride hard for the Wessex road, which ran between Nottingham and Gloucester. Ellie and Margery would share one horse, and Ralf would take the other. As Ellie checked her horse's saddle, Tom emerged from the hospital tent.

"I'm coming too," he said.

"Not with that broken arm, you aren't." She put her foot in a stirrup to test it.

"I said I'm coming." There was a hard command in his voice. He sounded like he had in the woods the day the sisters of Kirklees brought his uncle to them.

"It's too dangerous, Tom. You can't fight with your arm—you can barely *ride* with it."

He stared up at her, his gaze set and certain. "I'll come with you now or follow after you. Either way you can't stop me."

She got down from the horse, determined to make sense of Tom's secrets once and for all. "Who are you, Tom?"

"I've told you. My father is Lord—"

Ellie threw up a hand. "Don't tell me you're Lord Woodville's son, I know you're not. Tell me who you really are, and why you're so desperate to come with us."

"I can't."

"Does this have something to do with your uncle?"

"It would be disrespectful for you to push this any further." There was ice in his voice.

"You know you can trust me, don't you?"

Tom nodded. "Of course I do. But can't you trust *me*? Who I am doesn't matter now, and it won't hurt what you're trying to do."

Ellie considered for a moment. "If I let you come with us, will you promise to tell me after we're done? You're welcome to stay with the League of Archers—you can stay forever, if you like. But I don't think you want to. I think you want to go home. And if you tell me where your home is, I can help you get there."

A shadow seemed to pass over Tom's face. "I do want to go home," he said softly. "So very much. I'll tell you the truth after today. I promise."

Satisfied, Ellie helped the League continue their preparations. Margery nodded when Ellie told her Tom would be joining them, but Ralf looked at her askance.

"Seriously?" he said. "He could be just another Stephen."

Ellie glanced over to where Tom was fussing over one of the horses. "You really think so?"

Ralf sighed. "No. Not really. I don't know what to think anymore."

"He's loyal to us," she said. "We're all he has at the moment. He won't do anything to harm us, I know it."

They set off. As she watched Tom sitting behind Ralf, his back straight and his heels gripping the horse's flanks, it was obvious he'd grown up riding horses. But in whose house? Soon she would find out at last. The sun rose as they rode but didn't do much to strike through the chill, and their breath hung in misty clouds. From the edge of Sherwood they had a few hours' ride to the Wessex road.

They were far south when Ellie led them off the road. They continued their ride through fields and woods, not wanting to draw the attention of their quarry. At last they saw it: a dark wooden carriage, pulled by black horses kicking up dust from the road and surrounded by four mounted guards.

"That has to be it," said Ellie. "Let's get in front." They picked up speed until they'd left the coach behind. Not ten minutes later they reached a bend in the road.

"This is perfect!" Ellie said, marveling at their good luck. The coach would have to make a blind turn left where the path curved—and the League would be waiting just beyond it, to take the group by surprise.

They all dismounted, and Ellie and Tom led the horses away into the forest, where the trees grew less thickly and she could tie them up. "Stay with them," she told him. "We can't be worrying about you and that arm while we take on those guards." For a moment he looked like he was about to argue, but to her relief he just nodded.

She left Tom and settled in beside Ralf and Margery in the thick bushes by the bend, their bows at the ready. The sweat of travel was drying cold on her neck. In the distance came the rattle and thump of the coach drawing closer, while next to her she heard the rustle of Ralf and Margery settling down for the wait.

"Hey!"

Ellie stiffened. The frantic whisper was coming from the other side of the road.

"This is our raid! Get back to your tree house!"

Margery gasped and Ralf groaned in dismay. Ellie squinted at the bushes until she could see them: Stephen, Jacob, and Alice. Suddenly she felt cold all over.

"What are you doing here?" she snapped back angrily.

"You think you're the only one who knows about the circlet?" said Stephen. "Please. Everybody's talking about it. Now get out of here!"

"We're staying right where we are!" Ellie replied. "Go back to being Lord Clerebold's watchdogs. You're getting all the money you need from him, remember?"

"Alice, how could you?" Ralf broke in. "How could you work for a *lord*?"

"Leave her alone," Jacob hissed.

Alice turned on him. "Shut up, Jacob. You don't need to fight my battles."

"Stop it!" Ellie told them, as loudly as she dared. "Do you want the guards to hear you?"

"The circlet is ours," said Stephen. "Stop wasting our time and go!"

An arrow whizzed over Ellie's head, so close she could feel the draft it made blowing her hair. Alice's mouth snapped shut and Jacob looked pained.

Stephen nocked a second arrow to replace the one he'd just shot. "Remember, I only miss when I want to. That was your first warning and you won't get a second. Leave *now*."

Ralf was on his feet. He ran across the road, straight into the path of Stephen's arrow. The older boy's eyes widened, and for a horrible half second Ellie thought he might shoot—but he dropped his arm and scrambled up through the bushes. He and Ralf stood face-to-face in the road, barely a bow's length apart.

"You spoiled coward!" Ralf shoved Stephen in the chest, so hard he stumbled.

Stephen recovered and slammed Ralf in the shoulder. "You stupid little kid," he sneered. "Even your own sister doesn't want to be in your gang."

"Don't you dare speak for me," Alice growled from the trees. "Nobody fights for me, and nobody talks for me either."

The clatter of the approaching horses was loud now. The coach would be thundering around the bend at any moment, and Ellie knew that if she didn't do something, the chances any of them had of stealing the gold circlet would be gone forever. She sprinted into the road and grabbed Ralf by his jerkin. "Get back to the trees," she urged. "Before they see us!"

Ralf shrugged her off, still glaring at Stephen. Jacob ran out and grabbed Stephen's arm, but he shook Jacob off. And then it was too late: The coach came rattling into view.

The soldier in front, heavy with mail and wearing a crimson jerkin, yelled, "They're here!" and pulled his horse's head sharply to the right. As the animals and the carriage surged across the road, the League and the Merry Men scattered. The horses dragged to a stamping halt, and the four guards shouted out curses. Ellie shouldered her bow.

"The circlet," she cried to Ralf. "We can still get it!" She dodged between two of the mounted guards, Ralf on her heels.

"It's ours!" Stephen yelled.

Ellie ran for the carriage, trusting Ralf and Margery to deal with Stephen. Behind her came a coarse laugh. "They were right," said one of the soldiers. "This lot are just children."

With a wave of misgiving, Ellie realized that their presence hadn't surprised the soldiers at all. She pushed the thought aside, reaching for the carriage's dark wooden door. Behind her came the tooth-tingling sound of unsheathing swords.

"Attack!" the first soldier cried.

A guard leaped for her with shocking speed. He grabbed Ellie's shoulders, pulling her roughly away from the carriage. She fell hard to the ground. Another soldier slashed his sword at Ralf, the air whistling, but he just sidestepped away.

Ellie sprang to her feet, nocking an arrow, then sent it flying into the shoulder of the soldier who loomed over Ralf. Margery stood on one side of the road, Alice on the other, each trying to give Ralf cover with their arrows. Jacob's sword clashed against that of another soldier. Stephen was at the carriage door, trying to smash the lock with the hilt of his sword. With him out of the way, it almost felt like the League was fighting together again. The feeling gave Ellie hope.

A soldier was barreling toward her. She drew back, seeking the cover of the trees so she could arm her bow once more, then sent an arrow spinning into his leg. He yelped in pain.

Another figure joined the fray—and Ellie went cold. Tom had run out from the trees, awkwardly lofting the sword she'd made him carry, even though he could barely wield it with his one good arm.

"Tom, no!" Ellie screamed. "Get back to the horses!"

But it was too late: A soldier was bearing down on him. He was too fast and too close for Ellie to shoot without risking Tom's life. She kept her arrow locked on them, waiting for an opening—but, to her surprise, the soldier didn't strike a blow at Tom. He swept Tom up with one arm and pulled him, screaming, onto his horse.

"No!" Margery cried. "Let him go!"

The soldier cantered in a tight circle. Tom was thrashing in his grasp, but the man's arm was clamped firmly around him. The horse turned tail and galloped back up the road toward Nottingham, taking Tom with it.

Ellie watched them go, too shocked to move. The other soldiers began to fall back, and she realized with deadly certainty that their mission was now accomplished: They weren't escorting the circlet, but had lured the League here with the promise of it so they could snatch Tom. She wanted to howl with frustration—but that wouldn't help get Tom back.

"I'm going after him!" she yelled to Ralf.

She ran back into the gloom of the trees and untied one of the horses, her fingers clumsy with panic. She swung onto its back and guided it to the road. Two of the three remaining soldiers were injured and off their horses, and Stephen and Ralf were already back at each other's throats as Jacob and Alice fought with the third soldier. Ellie urged her horse into a gallop, leaving them all behind as she set off in hot pursuit of Tom and his kidnapper.

16

ELLIE HADN'T GROWN UP WITH HORSES AND, unlike Tom—or Stephen, she had to admit—wasn't a natural rider. She clung to the horse with her hands and knees, wondering every moment whether it might try to throw her off. She leaned forward over its neck, partly to hang grimly on, partly in the hope it would run faster.

The soldier and his mount were ahead. She could see that his horse was a tall, well-fed gray animal, and she caught a glimpse of Tom, still held firm in the man's grasp. But with every pace they were receding farther into the distance. By the time she turned onto the Kirklees road, they were almost out of sight entirely.

We're heading toward the Castle de Lays, she realized.

She wasn't even surprised. The baron had had something to do with the missing crown jewels, and a lot to do with the death of King John. It seemed inevitable that he should be behind Tom's kidnapping, too. After all, Tom had been with the League only because they'd saved him from the baron's clutches once before.

She dug her heels into her horse, willing it to go faster. She thought about the way the soldier had grabbed Tom without a second thought, the way he'd yelled, without surprise, "They're here!" Oh, the baron had set them up, she was certain of it.

That man who told Friar Tuck about the circlet—Edwin—was he in the baron's pay too, spreading rumors to trap us? Now, with the clear view of hindsight, it certainly seemed far too convenient that Tuck should wander into the Stag and Stoat and leave with information guaranteed to send the League rushing to the Wessex road.

It's exactly what we did when we thought the crown jewels were coming through Kirklees, she thought bitterly. *And the baron took the gamble that Tom would be with us.*

The gamble had paid off. They'd walked right into the baron's trap, like an intruder caught in one of the nets around the Greenwood Tree. She'd practically delivered the boy to his kidnapper. Her eyes burned with humiliation and regret.

The soldier, his horse, and Tom were just a speck on the road ahead. Ellie drew up the reins, easing her horse to slow down to a walk. The animal's breath came hot and fast, its back slippery with sweat. To carry on was pointless. She had no chance of catching them before they reached the baron's castle. *And I can hardly get Tom out of there by myself,* she thought. She dismounted and led her exhausted horse to a nearby stream. As it drank its fill, she heard the clatter of hooves and a coach. She drew back into the bushes and watched the three soldiers she'd last seen fighting the League come trotting past her. She held her bow ready, and even though one of them spotted her—his helmeted head whipping around, eyes meeting hers—they didn't slow.

They've already got what they came for, she thought. But what exactly was that? Who was Tom, and why was the baron so keen to make him his prisoner? Whatever the answer, he was clearly of far more importance than a gaggle of outlaws.

She rode slowly back to her friends, mindful of the exertions her horse had already made. They were still in the road. Jacob and Stephen were nose to nose with Ralf and Margery, all of them shouting. Alice was crouched by the verge, watching them moodily and toying with her knife.

"By the saints," Ellie muttered as she trotted up. She was sick of this arguing, sick of it to her core. She drew up to them and jumped down.

"Can you stop fighting for just five minutes!" she said. "Tom's gone, and it's our fault. It was a trap—the circlet was never coming here. Those men were working for your father"—she jabbed a finger at Stephen—"and lured us here so they could snatch him. Maybe if we'd been working together, instead of scrapping with each other, we could have stopped them."

Stephen gave a snort. "I'm sorry my father's got Tom, but do you think this changes anything?" He shook his head. "There's only room in Sherwood for one outlaw band, and it's not going to be led by a soft heart who's afraid to kill. Who doesn't even have the stomach to steal."

"Why do you think we came here?" Ellie found herself snarling. "To steal the circlet!" As Stephen scoffed in reply, Ellie cursed herself. Yes, she was sick of arguing, was ashamed that it had put Tom in such danger, yet here she was, at it again after just a few seconds. It seemed she couldn't even be near Stephen without boiling over like an unattended cooking pot.

"How did you know about the circlet, anyway?" Ralf demanded of Stephen. "Friar Tuck told us, and I don't see him talking to you."

Jacob looked sheepish.

"We were spying on you at the Greenwood Tree," Stephen said. "We were right there, listening to you make your plans. Some lookouts you've got—none of you even saw us."

"Oh, wonderful!" said Ralf. "So you're spies now? This gets worse and worse."

"What will you do next?" asked Ellie. "Steal from little children? Murder those who try to stop you? Where will it end, Stephen?"

He drew his sword. The rasp of metal cut through the arguing and made them all fall silent.

"Why not end it now, Ellie?" he said. His eyes flashed. "Finish it once and for all. The League of Archers versus the Merry Men."

Ellie's jaw dropped. She looked from Stephen's blade to his face, which was as hard as stone. Was he really suggesting that they fight?

Ralf and Alice were staring at each other mutely, the air crackling between them. Then Alice gave the tiniest shake of her head and shoved her knife back into her boot. Ellie knew that for Alice this gesture spoke volumes. She was refusing to fight against her brother.

Jacob let his bow fall to the ground. "I'm out too," he said quietly. "I can't fight my friends, Stephen. I just can't."

For a moment Stephen looked hurt. "Fine. Not one of you peasants knows how to wield a sword anyway. I'll take on the League of Archers by myself."

Ellie unhooked her bow from her shoulder. She reached back to her quiver and chose an arrow, carefully nocking it in place.

"If it's a fight you want, you'll get it," she said. "But not with the League of Archers—with me. And when I win, you'll leave us alone. All of us."

"So be it," said Stephen. "It's always been me against you, after all."

They circled each other, Stephen with his blade raised, Ellie sighting down her bow. She caught Ralf's anxious expression and wasn't surprised to see him worried— Stephen had proved in the fight when they rescued Tom that he was more than skilled with his sword. He'd seen battle, she knew, and not just skirmishes with the baron's guards—proper war, with hundreds of clashing knights. But she knew his weaknesses now too. He was reckless and he was arrogant. He was strong, but he didn't have her speed. And he didn't have his friends watching from the sidelines: Margery gripping the ends of her red hair, Jacob wearing a face like stone. Ralf with his arm around Alice, who watched Stephen with a malice that said she wished she were the one in the fight.

I can win this, Ellie thought.

Stephen lunged. The blade sliced close, nearly biting her arm, but she sidestepped just in time. Stephen struck again. Margery sucked in a breath as Ellie dodged. This time she stumbled a little, and Stephen surged forward to take advantage, striking quick and lower than she expected. She jumped over the swinging curve of his sword. Sprinting back a few paces, she recovered, and resighted her bow. But Stephen didn't stay still long enough for her to use it. The longbow was designed for distance; to hit a target close by was harder than it looked. What's more, Ellie knew that once she fired a shot, she would lose precious seconds reloading—precious seconds that Stephen could exploit.

Yet she wouldn't have wished for any other weapon in her hand. The bow had once belonged to Robin Hood. It had served him well, and she believed it would take care of her, too.

Stephen caught the front of her jerkin in a shallow swipe, but his shout of triumph cut off as she ducked behind him, leaving his back exposed. He spun around just in time, but she could see from the twist of his mouth that she'd shaken him. His determination was now tinged with frustration.

Getting to you, aren't I?

The rest of the League watched in perfect quiet as Ellie and Stephen almost danced on the road. The thrusts of his sword met the empty spaces where she'd darted out of the way. His sweeps were becoming wider, his footwork sloppy. He roared in frustration and lunged at Ellie— with such force that, as she nimbly dodged the blow, his own momentum carried him forward.

Ellie whipped around.

Now!

She fired. Her arrow shot clean through the fleshy part of Stephen's sword hand, between thumb and index finger. A fine spray of blood fizzed up. Stephen gave a hiss of pain. His sword fell with a clatter and he clutched his wounded hand to his chest. Ralf ran to collect his sword. The fight was over.

Stephen breathed heavily. His face was hard and proud. Ellie couldn't fault him for lack of bravery.

"That'll heal quickly," she said. "I missed the muscle and bone. Just wash and bandage it. That's what Sister Joan taught me." She lowered her bow and held out a hand. "You're not in the League of Archers," she said, "and you never will be. But if you stay out of our way, we'll stay out of yours. Agreed?"

Stephen glared at her. He seemed too stunned by his defeat to speak.

Disappointed, Ellie let her hand drop. "Come on," she called to her friends. "Let's go home and talk to Marian and Tuck. We need to find a way to rescue Tom."

They began to make their way to the horses. Then Margery screamed.

Ellie whirled around. Stephen had retrieved his bow and had an arrow leveled at Ellie's face. *He means to kill me.* The thought broke on her like a sweat.

He let the arrow fly.

Ellie bent out of his way one last time, the arrow flying so close she felt its breath on her hair. She heard the horrible slick sound of its tip meeting flesh, and the soft thump of a body falling to the earth.

Ellie turned. Alice lay on the ground, red running from her cheek into the dirt.

"Alice!" Ralf howled. He fell to the ground beside his sister.

Margery gave a terrible sob. "Is she . . ."

Ellie dropped down beside Ralf. To her infinite relief, Alice groaned and clutched at her face.

"Wait," she soothed, pulling Alice's fingers away. The arrow had left a long score across her cheek. An inch to the right, and it would've gone into her eye. She would have died like a rabbit, out here on the road. Ellie felt light-headed at the horror of what had so nearly happened.

"You could've killed her!" Ralf screamed. His face was twisted with rage. Margery was weeping, Jacob gawping at Stephen in disgust.

Stephen himself was as white as a ghost. "I didn't mean . . . I thought . . ."

"Go," Ellie growled at him. "If you ever set foot in Sherwood Forest again, I really will shoot you—and not just to wound. Do you understand me?"

He nodded, turned, and ran off down the road.

17

RALF RIPPED A STRIP OF FABRIC FROM HIS tunic and pressed it to his sister's cheek.

"Are you okay, Liss? Does it hurt?"

"Of course it hurts," Margery sobbed. "She got shot in the face with an arrow!"

"Quiet, Margery," said Jacob from where he hovered nervously behind them.

"It's true," Alice croaked. She propped herself up on her elbows. "I'm all right, Ralf, honest. I feel like I've stuck my head in a wasp's nest, but I'm okay." Some of the tension went out of Ralf's shoulders.

Ellie stood a little way apart from them. All she could think was that Stephen might have fired the shot, but ultimately it was because of her decisions that Alice was wounded on the ground, lucky to be alive. She'd brought a wolf into their midst. It had been with the right intentions, but he'd proved a wolf all the same.

"I should never have brought him to camp," she said abruptly. "If I hadn't insisted you let him stay . . ."

"We shouldn't have left the League of Archers," said Jacob. He turned anguished eyes on Ellie. "I'm so sorry. He just seemed . . . well, I got him all wrong. Can you forgive me?"

Ellie felt all the wrongs of the last few days righting themselves, felt the weave of the five of them resetting around her. It was like coming home to a place you thought you'd never see again.

"There's nothing to forgive," she told Jacob. "I missed you, you know? You too, Alice. So much."

Jacob looked at her almost shyly from under his lashes. "Am I . . . can I still be in the League of Archers?"

Alice got up carefully, pushing Ralf aside as he tried to help her. The bandage made a grimy stripe across her cheek. "And me, Ellie?"

Marian's words crossed Ellie's mind, the words she hadn't dared believe at the time. *Your friends will come back to you. They will. And you just have to open your heart enough to forgive them when they do.*

"Of course you're in the League. Both of you. Always."

For a moment the five of them stood quietly in the road. It didn't feel right, with Alice so newly hurt, but happiness bloomed in Ellie like snowdrops in midwinter.

"So what now?" Jacob asked, turning to Ellie eagerly. She was pretty sure that right now he'd put a jug on his head and sing a song if she asked him to.

"First we take Alice to Marian. Then we rescue Tom."

The baron wouldn't get away with this. Not while Ellie was alive to stop him—and while she had the League of Archers back by her side.

Alice was a very bad patient. After insisting all the way back to the Greenwood Tree that she didn't need any further nursing, she was finally cowed by Maid Marian, who took one look at her and hustled her into the hospital tent. She made no mention of why Alice had been away, or why she'd come back.

Jacob didn't get off so easily. His shoulders had climbed higher and higher with tension as they got closer to camp, and he dismounted from the horse he'd shared with Ralf as if he wished he were invisible. When Friar Tuck saw him, he gave a great "Hah!" and charged across the clearing. Minutes later Jacob was hard at work replenishing the store of arrows he'd helped Stephen steal.

Ellie and Ralf joined Alice in Marian's hospital tent. She cleaned the wound with boiled witch hazel and laid a clean strip of linen across it. Then she pulled out a pot of thick, smeary balm. The smell of it made Ellie's eyes water. "A gift from Sister Joan. It'll sting, but it should stop the scarring."

Alice ducked her head away. "I *want* the scar."

Marian raised her eyebrows, then laughed. "Spoken like a true outlaw."

Tuck peeked his head into the tent. "Jacob and Alice aren't the only defectors from that fool boy's gang—half the camp is back, led by the Galpins." He smiled wickedly. "It looks like the baron's son wasn't the leader they hoped he'd be."

Ellie went to the tent flap. Sure enough, villagers were streaming back in, all of them carrying bundles of belongings or children too small to tramp through the woods. Some of the little ones were already spreading out around the clearing, laughing and climbing over the tree's great roots. But the adults looked wrung out, as if they hadn't put their loads down once since they left the Greenwood Tree. Jacob ran to greet his parents. The returning villagers were happily reunited with those who'd stayed; only Donald, sitting on a log, looked sour to see the clearing fill up again.

With Alice attended to, Marian came to join Ellie. She gave her a knowing smile. "It's very easy to mistake force for bravery. I don't think they'll be doing that again. I'm so happy for you, my dear."

Ellie smiled back—but although things were slowly coming right, guilt still ate away at her. "I should have left Stephen in Nottingham," she sighed. "Then Alice wouldn't be hurt. Tom wouldn't be kidnapped. Jacob wouldn't feel so guilty—"

"A little guilt won't kill him," Marian interrupted tartly. "It isn't bad for a person to reflect on their mistakes."

She cut a look to where Alice sat on the edge of the bed, poking at her wound. Marian turned away just a bit.

"You were right to give Stephen a chance," Marian continued more softly. "You didn't make him do the things he did, and you couldn't have foreseen them." Her eyes went far away, and she worried the plain nun's ring she still wore on her finger. "Stephen is a troubled boy—you can see it in his eyes. I have sympathy for him still, despite all he's done. To grow up with the baron for a father, to be sent off to war so young . . ."

"We've fought too." It was Ralf, come over to join them. His face was sour. "It didn't make us like he is."

"You've seen fighting, Ralf," said Marian, "but you

haven't seen war, and I pray to God you never will. Nobody comes through it unchanged. I was the ward of King Richard the Lionheart in my youth, remember, and I saw what the Crusades did to him—"

A groan came from the other side of the tent.

"It's Tom's uncle!" called Alice. "I think he's waking up!"

They hurried over. Marian grabbed a skin of water and swept to the man's side. He was clutching the sheets, his limbs stirring.

"All right, it's all right," she said soothingly.

Slowly his eyes opened. He looked around the room, his expression one of alarm. He tried to sit up but slumped down again. "What is this place?" he rasped.

Ellie rushed to help Marian prop him up.

"You're safe here," Marian said. "Please don't be frightened. You're in Sherwood Forest, in the Greenwood Tree, under the protection of the League of Archers."

The man's eyes went wild. "What? No . . . I can't . . . the king! Where is the king?"

"Here, drink this." Marian held the water to his lips, but with a surge of strength he dashed it from her hand.

"Tell me where the king is!"

"The king is dead," Ellie said as gently as she could.

The man looked at her in blank horror. He clutched

his gray hair with his hands. Ellie glanced at Marian, who seemed as uncertain of what to do as she.

"He was poisoned," Ellie pressed on. "At a banquet at Nottingham Castle. I'm sorry, was he a friend of yours?"

The man slumped back. He drew in a long, shaky breath.

"Praise be to God. You speak of King John, do you not?"

Ellie and the others nodded.

"My name is William Marshall. I am regent to the king, who is yet too young to rule. I was traveling south with His Majesty to his coronation when we were attacked. I need to find him. . . ." But the speech had worn him out. He dropped onto the pillow, his breathing fast and shallow.

Shock ran through Ellie like fire. Ralf put a hand to his mouth.

"The king was with this man?" said Alice in a strangled voice. "But that means Tom—"

"Is the king of England," finished Ellie in awe.

"Good Lord," whispered Ralf.

They stared at one another for a moment, utterly shocked. Marian recovered first, hurrying to fetch Marshall more water. She helped the man drink, while Ellie and Ralf gathered pillows to prop him up so he could sit. All four of them waited in silence for him to continue his story. At last he put the empty skin aside.

"He told us he was called Tom Woodville," said Alice. "His . . . His Majesty did, I mean."

The man gave a rueful smile. "The Woodville family are good friends to the old king," he said. "His true name is Henry—or King Henry III, as he will soon be crowned." He leaned forward urgently. "And he *must* be crowned soon! It's vital that the French have no chance to interfere—or, even worse, the barons. It'll be civil war otherwise. Where is His Majesty? I must see him immediately. We have no time to lose."

Oh, God!

Ellie glanced at Ralf. He looked like he might be sick. The air in the tent felt too close, too hot. Here at last was the answer to Tom's—no, Henry's—secret, the reason why the baron had been so keen to capture him.

"I'm sorry," she said, her voice ragged. "We tried to keep him safe. But this morning he was kidnapped by Lord de Lays."

William Marshall gaped at her in horror. He flung off the sheets and tried to climb out of bed. Marian took him by the shoulders, pressing him back down.

"Let go of me—I must retrieve the king!"

"You're far too ill to do anything of the sort," Marian

said. "Perhaps when you're strong enough to overpower an old woman, we'll reconsider."

Marshall's eyes fell on Ellie. His body was weak, but his gaze was strong, holding her in a grip of steel. She could imagine him fiercely defending the young king's interests at court. She braced herself for a torrent of rebuke.

"You are Elinor Dray, are you not?" the man said shortly.

Ellie nodded in surprise.

"And you are Maid Marian?"

Marian nodded.

"I've heard of the League of Archers, Elinor Dray. I know you saved this woman from within the baron's own dungeons. You made fools of him and his men, and stopped them from murdering a fine woman." His breathing was rough again, his skin a terrible gray. "You must do the same for the king. You must save him, do you understand? All England depends on you."

Later, when Marshall was sleeping again—a true sleep, Marian said, the kind that would help him heal—Ellie and the League gathered in the topmost platform of the Greenwood Tree, out of earshot of the villagers milling below. Ellie quickly filled Jacob and Margery in on what they'd heard inside the hospital tent.

"He's the king?" squawked Jacob. He clutched his sandy hair. "But . . . I told him off for taking too much stew!"

"He'll make a good king, don't you think?" Margery kept saying, her hands clasped together. "Brave, sympathetic to outlaws—and he never complained about sleeping outside, even when we didn't have enough blankets."

"I'd have given him mine," Jacob said sorrowfully, "if I'd known he was the king. More blankets and more stew."

Alice scoffed. "Oh, don't be ridiculous, Jacob. He'll have all the blankets and stew he wants once he's back in his own castle. It's a good thing for royalty to live like we do for once."

"It'll probably make him a better king," reasoned Ralf. "Though I expect he'll pass a new law against blanket hoggers."

Jacob scowled.

"But what does the baron want with him?" wondered Margery. "He's not—he's not going to kill him, is he, like he did King John?"

"I don't think so," said Ellie quickly. "He managed to make John's murder look like an accident. If Tom—I mean, Henry—dies too, things will look really suspicious. No, I think he's got something else planned."

"I bet he's still working with the French," Ralf said. "He'll hand Tom over to them."

"Henry," corrected Alice. "We'd better get used to his proper name."

Ellie stared upward, letting the shifting leaves settle her thoughts. "So he kills the king to make way for his son, who's young enough that he's easy to capture—and boss around. But what next? What would the French give him in exchange for the heir to England's throne?"

"Not just money," Ralf guessed. "He's got enough of that—and enough villages to steal from if he needs more."

"Power, then," said Ellie. "Maybe they'd give him some extra baronies. They could offer him the whole of the north."

They looked at one another with wide eyes. Ellie imagined the baron's cruel rule reaching beyond the village, a black cloud spreading over the land.

"Whatever he's been promised, he's not having it." She slapped her hand on the platform for emphasis. "We need to get Tom—*Henry*, I mean—out of the castle. If we wait too long, they could take him to France or anywhere. William Marshall said there will be civil war if he isn't crowned soon."

Alice raised an eyebrow. "So we're breaking into the baron's castle again?"

"We got Marian out," reasoned Ralf. "We can get Henry out too."

Ellie nodded. "But it'll be different this time. The baron will be ready for us. He'll be *expecting* us to come."

Jacob frowned. "So what do we do?"

Ellie looked away.

There's only one thing I can think of. . . . But will they go for it?

"We need help," she said slowly. "Help from someone who knows the baron's castle inside and out."

Ralf stared at Ellie, eyes widening as realization dawned. "No way," he said. "Not him."

"We have to," said Ellie. "It's the only hope we have of rescuing Henry. We need Stephen's help."

18

"I CAN'T BELIEVE YOU'D TURN TO HIM," RALF said bitterly. "After what he did to Alice."

The rest of the League looked equally appalled. Ellie could hardly believe she was suggesting it either. Stephen had betrayed her trust, nearly split up the League forever, nearly killed Alice. . . . If there were anyone else in all of England to turn to instead, she would. But the baron had Henry—had *King Henry III*—and their best chance at getting him free lay with Stephen.

Color rose in Jacob's cheeks. "You can't mean that, Ellie. I don't want anything more to do with him!"

"Me neither," said Ralf. "Just look at Alice's cheek."

Alice herself frowned thoughtfully. "I'm alive, though,

aren't I? And it's our fault King Henry was taken. Mine and Jacob's. If we hadn't been fighting, we'd have had time to protect him. So now we have to do whatever it takes to get him back." She put her hands on her hips. "If that means asking Stephen for help, so be it."

Jacob ducked his head. Ralf's mouth set into a thin line.

"She's right," Margery said quietly. "You know she is."

Ralf looked at Ellie seriously. "You're our leader, Ellie. If you really think we should do this, I won't fight you on it. So?"

"So we do it," said Ellie. "And not just because Henry's the king—because he's our friend. I promised when I met him that I'd protect him. I failed. Now I have to make it right."

Ellie slept poorly that night. When the darkness finally thinned to gray, she left Alice and Margery sleeping in their tiny cabin in the boughs of the Greenwood Tree and rode out of the clearing on one of the horses—which had been dubbed Chestnut—toward the Wessex road. She'd told Stephen to stay out of Sherwood Forest, and remembering his pale, shaken face, she felt sure he would have done. Where would he be now? She just hoped it wasn't far from where they'd parted.

It was late morning by the time she was back at the bend

in the road where Stephen's Merry Men had deserted him. She rode past, looking out for places Stephen might now be living. The first village she reached barely deserved the name. A clutch of shabby buildings by the road, it was nearly lost in the straggling trees at the forest's edge. A man watched Ellie approach from his perch on a stump in front of a muddy cottage.

"What are you hunting, girl?" he croaked, using his pipe to point at Ellie's bow. "These are the king's woods, and he'll shoot you down if he sees you."

I don't think the king would mind. . . .

"Good morning, sir," she said. "I'm looking for someone—a tall boy of about fourteen, dressed in black. He'd have been carrying a sword. And wearing a cloak with a jeweled clasp, I think."

The old man shook his head. "Yours is the first new face I've seen today. In many days, in fact."

Ellie thanked him and kept on down the road. The next village was larger—a handful of houses with a church at their center, and what looked like a blacksmith's forge at its edge—but nobody there had seen Stephen either.

As she rode through two more villages without luck, the sky broke open at the seams. It dropped first a drizzle of gray rain, then a flood, which soaked her tunic to her body and made her horse duck his head against the onslaught.

When she reached the next village, damp and shivering, the daylight was fading. She ate a fistful of dried meat from her pack and let rainwater run into her mouth. Then she trotted down the washed-out road to the village's heart, where people were rushing to bring their laundry in from the rain. A woman ran across her path carrying a load of firewood, then stamped her foot in annoyance as half of it tumbled from her arms. Ellie hopped off Chestnut's back and rushed to help her. Chestnut stood under a tree with his head down, rain running off his flanks, as they made a run for the woman's door. Ellie helped deposit the wood just inside it.

"My thanks to you," the woman said, her voice almost lost in the howling wind. "Can I offer you anything? I don't have much, but you're welcome to a slice of bread and cup of broth."

"You're very kind, but no," said Ellie. "I wonder if you can help me, though. I'm looking for a boy a little older than me, with red hair and dressed in black. . . ."

"And wearing a fancy cloak, too, if I remember right." Ellie grinned in relief.

"That sword he carried makes him hard to forget. Is he from the new king, do you know? Or the baron?"

"He was once," said Ellie honestly, "but he's on his own now. Do you know where I could find him?"

The woman shook out her wet hair. "I don't, I'm afraid. I saw him passing through just before this rain came down."

Ellie turned this over. "Maybe he ran for shelter."

"Could have done. If he did, he'd likely be in there." She pointed at a stone building down the way, as tumble-down as the rest but a little larger. A wooden sign bearing the words THE MERRY MINSTREL and a painted flute hung over its door.

"Thank you!" Ellie said, leading Chestnut toward the tavern. She could hear the thump and clamor of the crowd even before she entered the Merry Minstrel. She tied Chestnut under the shelter outside and paused to twist her hair under her cap and draw up her collar, just in case anyone recognized the outlaw Elinor Dray. Then she opened the door.

Hollers and laughter hit her like a hot wave. The tavern was barely as large as the abbey kitchen, with tables and chairs crammed against the walls. But nearly every seat was empty. The crowd was instead gathered around a table at the very center, where two men sat across from each other, faces red, elbows planted hard on the tabletop—arm-wrestling. One was an older man with a nose like a rook's beak and a shock of silver hair. His skin looked tough as leather. Across from him, his back to Ellie, was a boy dressed in black, with a tumble of autumn-bright hair.

Stephen!

Ellie pushed through the eager crowds. The older man was big. But every sinew of Stephen's neck was taut with effort. Their hands, locked together above the center of the table, trembled back and forth. Stephen's was bound with a bandage, but he seemed untroubled by the wound Ellie had given him. With a roar he slammed the man's arm onto the table.

The noise in the room doubled. Some cheered in triumph, others groaned with defeat, money changing hands as the spectators made good on their bets. A round man with a hairless round face like a toad's grabbed Stephen's arm and held it high. "Another victory for the boy in black!" he croaked. Stephen turned slightly, and Ellie glimpsed that familiar, infuriating grin. "But!" The toadlike man stuck up a finger. "Will another contender end his winning streak? Place your bets! Next contender up!"

The men looked among themselves. A couple were shoved forward to the seat opposite Stephen but refused the challenge.

Impulsively Ellie raised her hand.

The toad-faced man squinted at her. Then he threw his head back, roaring laughter. "Place your bets, men! Somebody's daughter wants to try her hand!"

Laughter filled the tavern. "Good luck, lass," a man with a scrubby beard told her. "We'll make sure he don't hurt you!"

Ellie ignored them. She pushed through the grinning men, hooked her bow and quiver on the back of the chair across from Stephen, and sat down. He started. His pale-blue eyes went wide, the grin slipping off his face like butter sliding across a hot pan.

"*You?*" he growled. "What are you doing here?"

"I need to talk to you."

He gave a scornful laugh. "What's left to say? You told me you didn't want to see me again. So why don't you get lost?"

Ellie placed her elbow on the table, hand open. "All right, then. How about this—if I beat you, you'll listen to me?"

Stephen narrowed his eyes. He put his own elbow on the table and gripped her hand. "Fine."

He bore down on her palm, hard. But Ellie was ready for him and pressed back. The crowd roared in anticipation. "Bets are closed on this one," someone yelled.

"Odds are too heavily in favor of the boy in black." But as soon as Stephen's fingers had wrapped around hers, Ellie could tell she had a chance. If Stephen had been fresh—if he hadn't just wrestled several of the strongest men in this tavern—perhaps he would have beaten her right away. But he wasn't.

Their eyes met over their locked hands. Stephen looked determined and a little worried. She was sure he could feel the strength in her arm—strength she'd gained from climbing, from shooting, from carrying wood for fires and for building shelters. All the softness of her life at Kirklees Abbey had been burned away, leaving something hard and unyielding behind. Stephen's larger build might defeat her in the end, but she could hold him for a few minutes at least. The crowd seemed to sense the match was closer than they'd first thought, their roars becoming more excited. If Ellie could throw him off guard, she might even win.

"Remember Tom?" she said through gritted teeth, her words hidden under the crowd's whoops and cheers. "The boy your father kidnapped?"

Stephen grunted. "What of him?"

"He isn't really Tom Woodville. He's King Henry of England."

Stephen flinched. His arm wavered a moment.

"You must know what that means," she pressed in a hard whisper. "Your father will be rewarded by the French lords he's working for. He'll become even more powerful."

Stephen pressed on her hand so viciously, she nearly lost the fight right there. "Tell me why I should care."

Ellie's arm felt like it was on fire. She could feel sweat breaking out all over her body. "When you joined the League," she panted, "you said it was to get revenge against him. Didn't you?"

"Yeah, I did. And then you kicked me out."

Ellie bit back the stream of retorts that rose at that. "Do you still want revenge?"

Stephen's arm was slackening. He still held her off, but he wasn't concentrating on defeating her. He was too interested in what she had to say. And just as well—Ellie knew she couldn't last for much longer.

"Then help us get a revenge he'll never forget," she said as steadily as she could. "Stop your father's plans. Help us rescue the king."

A fine sheen of sweat broke on Stephen's forehead. He looked soft and searching for a moment, then his eyes hardened.

"No," he snapped. "I'm not like you. I don't help people. I just disappoint them."

The last was said with such disgust Ellie nearly lost her grip. She knew she had to think past her anger toward him, past Jacob's shame and Alice's injury. Marian had said Stephen couldn't help being troubled, that everyone deserved a chance. . . .

"That's not true," she said. Her arm was almost numb now. "You saved us that day. The day with the . . . the flaming arrows. We would've been captured otherwise. You saved Jacob's life, too, when we held up the carriage. Don't you see," she rushed on, "this is your chance to make amends for the rest of it? For trying to kill me. For hurting Alice."

He suddenly bore down so hard on her arm she wanted to scream, a fiery hatred in his eyes. Then he yanked his hand free.

Ellie slumped against the table. Her fingers were red raw. Stephen rubbed his own hand, his expression bleak—and Ellie knew, as certainly as she'd known anything, that the hatred he had was turned inward. On himself.

"A *draw*?" said the toad-faced man in mock alarm. "You couldn't beat a girl?"

"Not this one." Stephen scraped back his chair, wiping the sweat from his face.

A tall man grabbed at his shoulder. "I had good money riding on you," he growled. "Money on you winning the next five matches. Why'd you go soft on us?"

Wearily Stephen flipped him a coin. "My apologies. Buy yourself a drink."

He picked his way to a table in the corner of the tavern. Ellie grabbed her bow and arrows and followed. They sat down opposite each other once more, a serving woman bustling around them with bowls of stew and cups of wine. "On the house," she said. "Nothing gets them drinking like a bit of competition."

They ate in silence. The stew was turnip and some kind of meat Ellie couldn't identify, but after a day spent on the road it filled her up well enough. She felt strange sitting there with Stephen, eating supper at a table—it was like a glimpse into another life she might have led, one far removed from fighting and stealing. She stole a glance at him. The first time they met, that day at Nottingham Castle, he'd been so confident, his every move full of swagger, with a smile that came and went like sunshine on a cloudy day. Now, picking at his food, he looked sad and tired.

She put down her spoon. "Stephen, you talked about disappointing people. You didn't just mean the League, did you?"

"Isn't that enough?" he muttered. He fiddled with a loose thread on his black jerkin, the pattern embroidered on it now tattered.

"I think you were you talking about your father."

He pushed away his bowl and stared through the window at the darkness and rain. "I didn't always know what he was. I thought he was worth impressing, once. A long time ago."

"Is that why you went to the Crusades?"

He didn't seem to have heard her. "Nothing worked. None of it. Everything I did to make him proud, he acted like it was nothing. So I became a squire. I thought I was ready. That I'd make him glad I was his son." He gave a laugh, as cold as winter snow. "I loved it at first—the armor, the knights, everyone looking forward to glorious victory. What an idiot I was. I had no idea what I was getting into. I saw . . . I saw terrible things. . . ." He seemed to see them then, like ghosts hovering just beyond her shoulder. He seized his cup and gulped down half of it. "Then we were captured, my knight and I. That prison— my God. I thought I'd died and been sent to hell. And when I managed to escape, when I found my way back to England, do you know what my father said? That I was a coward for running away. He told me he'd rather I'd died on the battlefield than skulked home like a whipped dog."

Ellie stared at him in horror. She thought of her mother, who used to sing to her when she scraped her knees. And farther back, of her own father. His face was fading, but she could still see it sometimes, right before she fell asleep. He used to lift her onto his shoulders when she cried, to make her laugh. She couldn't understand a father who would send his child away to war, then have no sympathy for what he'd endured, but mock him instead. She thought of William Marshall lying wounded in the clearing, and Stephen's strange reaction to him. Little wonder he had been so horrified, had wanted to stop them starting a hospital. Every day he would be faced with a terrible reminder of the Crusades.

"It's your father who should be ashamed," she said. "Not you. For sending you to battle, for trying to kill Marian. For using Henry as his pawn." She leaned forward to make him look her in the eye. "Help us, Stephen. Do the right thing, and you'll prove to your father you're the better man. Because you can be. You are."

Stephen pushed back his chair and turned away from her. Ellie knew it would take him more than a moment to decide. But time wasn't on their side. She just had to hope he'd make the right decision. And quickly.

19

TAX DAY AT THE CASTLE DE LAYS HAD A FUNEREAL
air. The baron's courtyard was as crowded as if it were
a holiday, but everyone's head was down. No laughter
broke the air, and what talk there was sounded subdued.
People clutched sacks of grain or led animals on ropes,
watching with hungry eyes as the baron's well-fed men
looked over their spoils. Everywhere was a feeling of
defeat.

Because they didn't have grain or animals they were
prepared to hand over, the League were carrying stacks of
firewood to give to the baron as tax. Hidden among them
were their bows and arrows.

Stephen was with them. In the end it hadn't taken him

long to decide whether he would help them rescue King Henry from his father—just a short solitary walk and a small cup of weak ale. Instead of the stolen jeweled cloak, he wore a shabby brown one, the hood up to cover his red hair.

"I still don't trust him." Ralf was looking straight at Stephen, not making any effort to lower his voice.

Stephen said nothing. He'd given the League a quick nod of greeting when they met at the edge of the baron's lands that morning, and barely spoken at all. His eyes kept skating over Alice's cheek, then darting away.

"Well, I *do* trust him," Ellie insisted. *Maybe if I keep saying so, he'll live up to it.* "Remember, we're not using violence," she continued, looking at him pointedly. "Remember the plan. Stephen will distract the baron, then come and meet us in the courtyard."

They filed with the rest of the crowd into the baron's great hall, keeping their hoods pulled up close around their faces. The room was huge, the ceiling supported by columns of wood, with straw scattered over the stone floor. The smells of smoke, sweat, and charred meat swept Ellie back to the first time she was here—as the baron's prisoner, alongside Maid Marian. And the second time, when she and the League had rescued Marian from his grasp. Her heart beat faster. The League had nearly

THE STOLEN CROWN

died that day. They'd escaped only because they'd taken the baron by surprise, and because Friar Tuck and an army of villagers had come to their aid. Would they be so lucky today? *The baron must know we're coming,* she thought grimly. *He must realize I wouldn't just let him take the king.*

The League joined the line of villagers waiting to make their payment of grain or animals. The line snaked toward a long table where, on a high-backed chair, sat Lord de Lays. Beside him was a rotund man with a circle of hair around a bald spot, like grass around a lake, his nose bent over a pile of parchment.

"Tax records," Stephen muttered. "That's Roger Bruton, my father's scribe. A thief, just like my father, but mostly from the kitchen."

The baron wore a cloak of green velvet, his pointed black beard neatly trimmed. From a silver pitcher he poured himself a goblet of wine, the gaudy rings on his fingers clanking on the metal. The contrast he made with the ragged, hungry people winding through the great hall filled Ellie with the kind of feelings Sister Joan would advise her to pray away.

The baron's blue eyes, so much like his son's, scoured a sheet of parchment. "Hugo Ingram," he read. "Come forward."

A man with thin white hair shuffled deferentially to the

236

table. A soldier prodded him with the hilt of his sword, and he stumbled the rest of the way. Roger Bruton, the scribe, whispered in the baron's ear. The baron grinned nastily.

"You, Hugo Ingram," said Lord de Lays, "owe me a groat."

The old man gaped, showing missing teeth. "A . . . a groat?" he said. "If you please, sire, it was but two pennies on the last tax day." He scrounged in the pocket of his cloak and pulled out two grubby coins. "I have them here."

The baron's face darkened. "Can you not understand me, old man?" he said. "Have you been so long in the company of your pigs that you've lost the capacity for human speech? You owe me a groat. Pay quickly, or pay the price."

"Please, sire." The man was very close to tears; his voice clawed at Ellie. "I have nothing left to give. I had to go hungry to get these." He held out the pennies. "Please take them. Please show mercy."

The baron took a lazy sip of his wine. "Lock him up."

Two soldiers grabbed the man by the elbows and dragged him from the room. Ellie caught sight of the old man's face, twisted with shock. A few gasps and murmurs went up from the crowd, but nobody tried to help him. It took everything Ellie had to hold back from interfering, because to do so would be to give themselves away. *Save the king first,* she told herself. *Then we can help these people.*

The scribe dipped a quill into an inkpot and scribbled on the tax records. The baron was looking down at his parchment to see who would be called forward next. Ellie felt Stephen's eyes on her. She turned to him and he raised his eyebrows questioningly.

She nodded. *Yes, now.*

The baron opened his mouth to summon the next villager—and froze. Stephen was marching toward him, hood thrown back.

"Good day to you, Father," he said.

The words dropped like stones in water. The baron pushed himself up from the table, scattering sheets of parchment and knocking over his goblet of wine. The scribe frantically moved his tax records away from the spreading red puddle.

The baron came to stand face-to-face with his son. His expression was shocked, all the conniving and arrogance having dropped away. He looked like a different man in their absence.

"Stephen," he said softly. "You're back."

Murmurs rippled through the great hall. "Is that Stephen de Lays?" an old man near Ellie whispered. "I heard he'd run off to be an outlaw!"

The baron raised his hand, touched Stephen's cheek briefly, then pulled away. "Where have you been?" he asked. His voice was hard again.

"I've just escaped, Father." He sounded as coldly composed as the baron. "From the League of Archers."

His father's face twisted with disgust. "You were with the League of Archers?" His voice rose—he clearly didn't care if the whole of the castle heard him. "It was the girl who took you, wasn't it? The outlaw Elinor Dray?"

"Yes. The girl, they say, who killed Robin Hood. The same girl who freed Maid Marian from your dungeons."

Gasps sounded around the room. Ellie held her breath—baiting the baron by reminding him of his failures wasn't part of the plan, and she hoped Stephen wouldn't push his father too far.

"She led me from Nottingham at knifepoint," Stephen went on. "The League wanted to hold me for ransom, but I fought my way free instead. I told them you'd never pay it. That you'd never negotiate with outlaw scum."

The baron smiled, but not kindly. "Kidnapped, indeed? Are you sure you didn't just run away? After all, you have a history of doing that."

Stephen's fists clenched. For a horrible moment Ellie thought he might turn on his father and ruin everything. She caught Ralf's eye, his expression tense.

But Stephen knelt before the baron, his head bowed. "I would never run away, Father. Not again. Punish me if you must, but I speak the truth."

Ellie let out a breath. In that moment she knew they could trust him. Maybe not before, and perhaps never again after, but right now, in their plot to save Henry from his father, he was their ally.

Lord de Lays looked mollified. He gestured to Stephen to get up. "We will resume tax collection tomorrow," he announced to the great hall. "Whoever hasn't paid his debts shall return in the morning. Come, Stephen. We have much to discuss."

The great hall erupted in a babble of amazed chatter. The scribe started gathering up the parchments as the baron swept from the room, Stephen hurrying in his wake. He glanced at Ellie as he passed, his lips quirking in a small but triumphant smile.

Please let him be careful, Ellie thought. *We're lost if he isn't.*

The League gathered together, shifting their piles of firewood. "Well," said Margery, "at least the baron's pleased to have him back."

Alice snorted. "He'd have been just as happy if someone had brought him an extra candlestick."

"Poor Stephen," said Ralf. "I almost feel sorry for him. Our plan's got off to a good start, though."

They joined the rest of the crowd, making their way back out to the courtyard. It thronged with villagers and the usual business of the castle—servants and soldiers hurrying to and fro, bearing loads of laundry or bossing the crowd. The League dispersed among them, as they'd agreed, like deer scattering at the cries of a hunt; they'd be less noticeable by themselves than if they stayed in a group. Ellie found a place next to a cart filled with hay. She ducked behind it, dropping her load of firewood and sliding out her bow and arrows. She concealed them under her cloak. All around the courtyard, she knew, the rest of the League would be doing the same.

She stepped out and scanned her surroundings. The first time they infiltrated the baron's dungeons, to rescue Marian, they'd found an inner entrance. Stephen had told them about another way they should use this time, and Ellie saw it now—just before the portcullis, the huge metal grille that separated the courtyard from the bridge, which extended over the moat of water encircling the castle.

"It'll be guarded," Stephen had told them briefly that morning, "but by no more than two men. They change shifts three times a day, and that's when we should strike. Wait for me and I'll show you into the dungeons."

"Wait where exactly?" Alice had demanded. "Where are we supposed to hide?"

He'd shrugged. "In plain sight, of course. All you need to do is blend in."

And so far, so good, Ellie thought. She could see the rest of the League, dotted around the courtyard, no one taking any notice of them. She left the cart and passed close, but not too close, to the portcullis. The door beside it was made of heavy wood reinforced with bars of iron. Two soldiers stood by it, just as Stephen had said. One was leaning against the wall, looking half-asleep. The other was grinning at a pretty serving girl.

Not exactly crack troops, Ellie thought. Hope bloomed inside her. She tramped past the dungeon door and found a discarded sack of seed. She fed them to a gaggle of hens pecking around in the dust, keeping an eye on the soldiers and watching for Stephen. Margery was in the opposite corner of the courtyard, pulling up weeds, while Alice and Jacob had found buckets from somewhere and were carrying them back and forth. After a while the chickens lost interest in the seed. Ellie started to wonder what was taking Stephen so long.

Ralf strolled over, a broom slung over his shoulder. "Still no sign of him?" he asked Ellie out of the side of his mouth.

"Not yet."

"He said he'd find us as soon as he could. What could be keeping him?"

Ellie ran through the possibilities in her head. The baron had figured out the truth and had thrown Stephen in the dungeons. The baron had believed him, but Stephen couldn't safely get away. The baron *hadn't* believed him and was now torturing him into telling the truth.

"I don't know," she told Ralf. "But I'm telling you, I trust him. He'll be here."

Ralf looked like he wanted to say something to that, but shook his head instead.

Two guards came marching across the yard, spears in one hand, swords hanging from the belts that circled their chain mail tunics. Ralf dropped his broom and seized Ellie's bag of seed, throwing handfuls at the chickens.

"Eat up, chickens," he said loudly.

Ellie elbowed him. "Look! They're changing shifts!" she hissed.

The men at the dungeon door stirred from their positions. "You're late," said the half-asleep one. "You think I'm standing here for a laugh?" The other gave the serving girl a regretful shrug.

"It's you who was late this morning," his replacement replied. "Now move along. You've got drinking to do, don't you?"

"What's that supposed to mean?" retorted the first soldier, squaring up to him.

Ellie glanced around—yes, the rest of the League had seen what was happening too. Jacob and Alice came closer with their buckets. Margery stood, brushing the earth from her knees.

But where's Stephen?

The four guards were bickering irritably right beside the door. They seemed distracted enough for the League to fight past, but with no Stephen, how would they know where to find Henry? *And we haven't got a backup plan. . . .*

"Come on," she muttered to Ralf. She pulled the hood closer around her face and crossed the courtyard, hoping a plan would materialize by the time she reached the other side.

A hand grabbed her wrist, wrenching her back. She gasped, immediately reaching beneath her cloak for her bow.

"Don't," her assailant whispered. "The whole courtyard will see."

Ellie breathed out. It was Stephen.

"What took you so long?" she asked quietly.

"The king's not in the dungeons."

Ellie squeezed her eyes shut. "We're too late?"

"He's not gone. He's up there."

Ellie turned just enough to see him. He had the brown cloak on again, his red hair hidden. His eyes darted up—and up. . . . Ellie followed his gaze to the castle's highest tower. It was a narrow black shape, outlined by sun, a row of battlements on the top like an ogre's teeth. Ralf had followed Stephen's gaze too and let out a groan.

"Father didn't think he should put a king in a prison cell," Stephen murmured. "So he's in a bedchamber up there. Still under lock and key, of course."

The tower was even taller than the Greenwood Tree. Arrow slits were cut into the walls, and at the top was a window—and on the other side of the glass, Ellie imagined, sat poor Henry.

"So how," she said slowly, "are we going to get all the way up there to save the king from your father's hospitality?"

Stephen gave a grin—one of his old, arrogant ones. "Lucky you've got me with you, isn't it? Follow behind, but keep your distance. I can't help you if you get caught."

Ellie and Ralf trailed Stephen through the courtyard. She gave a jerk of her head, indicating to the others to follow too. To her relief, they did. Stephen led them past a large puddle a few muddy children were splashing their feet in, and around two stamping horses being brushed by a pair of bored grooms. Ralf skidded in a pile of dung, which made a small boy shriek with laughter—but apart from that, nobody took any notice of the six hooded figures making their way toward the castle tower. Stephen swung open a door in the side of the keep, pausing briefly to make sure they were still behind him, then led them down a passageway running the length of the castle. It spat them out onto a small square of grass. Above them, looming up into the sky, was the tower.

"There," Stephen said, pointing up.

Ellie looked at him, looked up. "What?"

"Henry's window. It's open." He smiled at her again. She saw flashes of the swaggering boy he'd been the day she met him. She wasn't completely sorry for it. "Don't you remember how we got out of Nottingham Castle?" he asked. "Now we just have to do the same thing . . . but in reverse."

"Coming down and out is one thing," Ellie said. "Getting up and in is another thing entirely! How would we . . ."

She trailed off as she saw the length of rope in Stephen's hand.

"I had to search for this—it's what took me so long.

Now we just need your arrow." He held out the rope to her. Ellie looked from it to him to the anxious faces of the League.

"Don't be ridiculous," she told Stephen. "Maybe I could get an arrow through the window, but with rope attached? That would change the balance of the shaft completely. Wouldn't it?" she said, appealing to the League.

Jacob pursed his lips thoughtfully. "I don't know, Ellie. I think you've got a chance." Margery nodded eagerly.

"You won't know until you try, will you?" said Alice.

"You know you can do it," said Stephen. "You're the best shot here. Better than me."

"He's right," said Ralf. He waved them all back. "Come on, give Ellie room."

She readied her bow, lifted an arrow from her quiver. The plan was a mad one, yet she could see it was their only chance. Her heart began to beat a little faster. She began tying the rope to the arrow, then changed her mind and returned it to her quiver. Instead she drew out another—a slender, shining thing that shone in the sun. She'd almost forgotten it was there.

"Oh," Margery breathed. "That's Robin's arrow, isn't it? The one he won from the Sheriff of Nottingham."

Ellie shook her head. "I gave that one to Marian for

safekeeping. This is its twin—it belongs to the sheriff himself. Or at least it did until I stole it from his chambers."

Alice laughed. "You didn't!"

"That's perfect," said Ralf, grinning. "The plot to kidnap Henry started in the sheriff's castle, didn't it? It's right that his arrow should end it."

Ellie nodded. A shiver passed through her. In silence she knotted the rope to the arrow's end, then hefted it in her hand a few times, trying to understand its new weight. She nocked it, squinting upward at the open window. "I hope Henry is standing well clear," she murmured, between a wish and a prayer.

Then she aimed high.

And fired.

20

THE ARROW FLEW HIGH AND STRAIGHT, CARRYING
the rope behind it. Ellie watched, stomach churning,
cursing herself every second for getting the shot wrong,
for sending the silver arrow and their only length of
rope into the wall below the window or into the air
above it. . . .

The arrow arced, the rope snapping behind it, dipped
down—and soared cleanly through the cell window.

"Yes!" whooped Ralf, grabbing Ellie in a hug. Alice
punched the air, while Margery and Jacob cheered.
Relief flooded through Ellie. She caught Stephen's eye;
he raised his eyebrows in a *Told you so* expression, and for
once she didn't even mind.

A face appeared at the cell window.

Henry!

The young king had the silver arrow in his hand. He was very high up, yet Ellie could still make out his expression—confusion that slid into elation. He grinned down at them and they grinned back. Henry drew the rest of the rope up through the window, then mimed tying a knot. His head withdrew again.

"Nice shot," Stephen said, arms folded across his chest.

"It was better than a nice shot," Jacob said. "Best shot I've ever seen, Ellie!"

Henry reappeared. He tossed down one end of the rope, which tumbled in coils to the ground. The other end held fast, clearly tied to something by the window. He gave it a yank with his left arm, looked uncertainly toward the ground, and hoisted one leg over the sill.

"Wait!" Ellie cried as loudly as she dared, waving her arms at Henry. He froze. "He can't climb down with that broken arm," she said to the others. To Henry, she called, "I'll climb up and help you!" He nodded and climbed back into the cell once more.

Ellie turned to Stephen, heart thumping. "Once I've got him down, do you have a plan to get us out of here?"

Stephen gave another wide grin. "How could you ever doubt me?"

Jacob snorted. "Yeah, I wonder why. . . ."

"Well?" Ellie said impatiently.

"I'll pretend I'm going riding," said Stephen, "and bring a horse around from the stable. Henry's little enough to hide under my cloak, but the rest of you will have to sneak out on your own. You've gotten out of worse situations, I'm sure." Then he winked and strode back toward the courtyard.

Margery shook her head as she watched him go. "Every time I start to think he's all right . . . ," she muttered.

"I've never thought he was all right," Ralf retorted.

Ellie shucked off her cloak and grabbed the rope. The window looked farther away than it had a moment before. "I'll be up and down again as quick as I can. Keep watch."

The patch of grass they stood on was secluded and unkempt, with no entrance but the one they'd come by. Henry's window faced away from the baron's great courtyard, but she could still be spotted as she climbed—by one of the guards circling the perimeter of the moat, perhaps. A guard who might be carrying a bow and arrows, watching for outlaws scaling the castle walls. She pushed the thought away.

"If you're halfway up the wall and someone comes, we'll do more than keep watch," Alice said, gripping her bow. The wound on her cheek had clotted, and she'd pulled off the bandage. She looked like someone you wouldn't want to argue with.

Ellie turned back to the wall, forcing her gaze not to climb skyward. *Just one step at a time,* she told herself. She'd climbed down from Nottingham Castle, and she could climb up the Castle de Lays. Her bow a familiar weight on her shoulder, she began her ascent.

She pulled herself up with the rope, hand over hand, her feet searching for footholds in the crooked stone wall. When she slipped, her knees and elbows scraped painfully against it. Ignoring the strain in her shoulders and the burn in her hands, she climbed steadily upward. She didn't let herself look down, yet could sense the ground getting farther away, the sounds of the castle courtyard fading beneath her. She dared a look upward once or twice, spying Henry's worried face peering down at her.

At last she was there, scrabbling for the windowsill, Henry doing his best to heave her over with his one good arm.

"You came!" he said, dazed. "You came to save me!"

Ellie spilled into the room and hugged him. "Of course we did," she said—then remembered she was speaking to a king and let go. "Of course, Your Majesty."

The boy's eyes widened. "How did you . . ."

"Your uncle—well, William Marshall, your regent—he woke up."

Henry grasped her hands in his. "How is he?"

"He'll live, Your Majesty."

He grinned and Ellie's awkwardness melted away. He was still the same boy she'd pulled frightened from the carriage, whom she'd taught to hunt.

"I am so grateful to all of you," Henry said. "I'll never forget what you've done for me. For my kingdom."

"The League is loyal to its members. Especially when they turn out to be royalty."

Henry laughed, then became serious again. "I'm sorry I didn't tell you the truth. I didn't dare say anything that might get back to Lord de Lays." He sighed. "But he found me anyway."

Ellie wanted to tell him she was sorry, for not keeping her promise to keep him safe from the baron. She wanted to tell him she almost wished he *were* Tom, not the king, because then she could ask him to stay with them in Sherwood Forest. But there was no time for that now.

"Here," she said, holding up the rope and surveying Henry. "I'm going to tie this to you and lower you down."

He looked at her doubtfully. "Like a bucket?"

"I'm sorry, Your Majesty, but yes. Like a bucket."

He grinned again and lifted his arms, letting her draw up the rope and knot it tightly over his chest. "Brace your feet against the wall and hold the rope with your good arm," she said as she helped him over the sill. He looked down, fear flickering over his face for just a moment. Then his self-command returned and his sharp little features set with determination.

"I won't let you fall," Ellie said. She began slowly to lower him, every muscle straining.

Don't drop the king of England. Don't drop the king of England!

Down, down, down he went—exactly, as Henry had said, like a bucket going down a well. On the ground the League of Archers anxiously watched his descent. As soon as they could reach, Ralf and Jacob lifted Henry down to the ground. Margery hurriedly untied the rope. Exhausted, Ellie let the rope hang limply over the window frame, leaning against the sill to rest her quivering limbs.

"Come on!" Ralf's cry drifted up to her. Alice waved her arms, beckoning Ellie down. She breathed deeply, spat on her hands for grip, and took hold of the rope once more. She swung onto the sill, hoping her arms wouldn't simply give way.

There was a flurry of movement on the ground. Alice was waving at her again, more frantically this time; Ralf, too. Margery grabbed Ellie's abandoned cloak from the ground, throwing it over Henry and pulling up the hood. Jacob had moved away, toward the door through which Stephen had led them.

Spilling from it were around twenty soldiers.

Ellie's heart plummeted. *They mustn't see the rope, or they'll know. . . .*

There was no time to pull it up. Nearly without thought, she drew an arrow from her quiver and with its head sliced the rope clean through. It tumbled to the ground. She felt sick watching it fall, taking with it her chance of escape.

Drawing to the side of the window, so she couldn't be spied from the ground, she watched with helpless horror the scene playing out below. Alice kicked the rope into a pile of brambles. Margery and Ralf stood in front of Henry. Jacob was saying something to the soldiers, clearly trying to buy time—something that annoyed one of them, as he raised a hand to swat him away. Jacob ducked the blow and rejoined the others.

The soldiers filled up the tiny yard, bristling with armor. "I said, what are you doing here?" the angry soldier demanded.

Alice's giggle sounded high and silvery—not like Alice at all. "Oh, well, we're paying our taxes, of course! But we got a bit lost after."

"Thank you for finding us," said Ralf with forced cheerfulness. "We'd have been stuck here all day."

A silence followed. None of the soldiers looked up at the

tower window, and Ellie wondered if they even knew where the king was being kept. The baron was certainly clever enough to keep his royal hostage's whereabouts secret.

"Come back tomorrow," one of the soldiers said finally. "And next time get off the baron's property when you're told to."

"Yes, sir," said Alice. They trooped off into the passageway, Henry in their midst, shrouded in the cloak. Ralf threw a last, worried look at the window before disappearing. The soldiers tramped out after them.

Ellie turned away and pressed her back against the cell's cool stone. Her friends had a good chance of escaping, she knew. Most likely they would be back at the Greenwood Tree before dark. King Henry would be safe—but Ellie had just taken his place as the baron's prisoner.

21

AT FIRST ELLIE COULDN'T SEE STRAIGHT. THE cell was just a blur of heavy furnishings and firelight, filled with the underwater sound of her own racing heart. She rubbed her eyes and forced herself to focus.

"What would Robin do?" she whispered.

Find a way out, that's what.

And if there was no way out, he'd make a plan.

The cell was circular, with two windows: the one she'd climbed into and another overlooking the courtyard on the other side. Set in the wall was a heavy wooden door secured with a lock larger than her fist. She resisted throwing herself against it—any guards stationed outside would be sure to hear the rattle.

The room was as opulent as anything she'd seen in the sheriff's chambers at Nottingham Castle. If it weren't for the lock, she would have believed Henry to be the baron's honored guest, not his hostage. Tapestries showing lords and ladies at a feast hung bright on the walls, and there was a great bed surrounded by curtains of purple silk. On a table before the fire lay parchment and a quill, a Bible, a plate with a half-eaten slice of cherry tart, and an empty goblet. Ellie's eyes ticked toward the door. Someone would be here soon, she was certain—to check on Henry, to take the plate away, to bring more food.

And what would the baron do when he discovered her in his hostage's place? The thought—of the moment of discovery, and the baron's rage—filled her with satisfaction. But thinking of what would come after—a proper dungeon cell, dark and dank and overrun with rats, and a trip to the gallows and the hangman—made her slump to the floor. When Robin Hood was murdered, the baron used Ellie as a pawn, pinning the crime on her. And here she was again, delivered to him as a convenient explanation for the king's disappearance. When the people were told she'd killed Robin, they'd hated her. If they thought she'd harmed the new boy king, they'd probably hang her themselves.

A creak came from the other side of the door. Her breath caught in her throat. She got up, crept over to it, and pressed her ear to the wood. The unmistakable clank of armor seeped through. Then the low rumble of a voice, and another one in response. So two guards at least.

Their presence stirred her to action. She hurried to pick up the silver arrow, which lay by the window, and slotted it into her quiver. She fixed an ordinary one to her bow. If there were just one guard, she could shoot him the moment he opened the door. With two . . . she'd have to hope the element of surprise would afford her enough time to dispatch them both. *And after that I'll just have to try fighting my way out of the castle. . . .*

A cold feeling went through her. If children years from now played at being the outlaw Elinor Dray, just as she'd once played at being Robin Hood, this might be the last tale told about her. She couldn't see a happy ending to this story.

A yell from outside the tower made her startle.

I know that voice!

She ran first to the window she'd climbed through, but the grass below was empty. She ran to the other window, the one that overlooked the courtyard. There she saw him—Ralf, a sword in his hand. Jacob, Alice, and Margery were there too, all armed. With relief she realized she couldn't see Henry. Had they managed to hide him somewhere safe?

But the League . . . Ralf's sword flashed in the sun as it struck Jacob's. Ellie's stomach turned to stone. What had Stephen done to set them against each other? Then Margery took a swing at Alice, who staggered dramatically backward. Suddenly Ellie pressed her hands to her mouth, suppressing a laugh.

The day Alice took a hit and didn't come back swinging was the day Ellie took up arms for the baron. They weren't fighting, they were creating a diversion!

But the distance from the top of the tower to the courtyard might as well have been miles. How could a fight down there help her up here?

As she watched, Jacob scooped up a horse pat in one hand and lobbed it at Ralf's head. Ralf ducked and the manure sailed on, hitting a guard square in the chest. The guard roared. Jacob dodged away from him, laughing. The guard accidentally sideswiped a boy carrying a grain sack, Alice took a wild swing that had her stepping on a villager's toes, and Margery shoved a girl—Ellie recognized her as the maid who had been flirting with one of the soldiers—into a puddle. The fight spread, infecting the courtyard like a plague.

Maybe it'll help me after all. . . .

She darted to the door, straining her ear toward what was happening on the other side. For a moment, nothing. Then, "Look, out in the yard!" one of the guards shouted. The clank and patter of them moving away from the door was followed by a low whistle.

"They've gone mad," another guard said wonderingly. "Think it's to do with tax day? The poor souls the baron threw in prison?"

"Shh!" the first guard said. "You better not call them that if you want to keep your position. They're officially thieves and criminals, remember, even if we know different. Come on, we'd better go see what the trouble is."

Ellie listened with rising hope as their footsteps moved away and out of earshot. She turned back to the room, looking around with wild eyes for the heaviest thing she could find. She almost laughed aloud when she spotted it: a stone bust of the baron himself, capturing every curve of his heavy face and each hair of his pointed beard. "It's too perfect," she said aloud.

Lifting it with both hands, she slammed the bust against the lock, again, again, bashing her fingers and biting her lip against the pain. The lock shuddered but it didn't give. Ellie went for the wood around it instead, the bust growing slippery with sweat as she swung. Finally the door splintered and the lock snapped free. Sagging with relief, she dropped the bust and it smashed into fragments on the stone floor.

Ellie seized a red velvet cloak from where it lay draped across the bed, wrapped it close around her to hide her face, and stomped over the broken pieces of the baron and out of the cell.

The hall outside was tiny, with just a stone bench beneath the window the guards must have looked through. Opposite was a stone staircase that wound out of sight. Holding the cloak's hood in one hand, and her bow in the other, Ellie ran down it. The staircase was dark, barely lit by the arrow slits cut into the walls; they were, she knew, designed for archers to fire through rather than scenic views. The castle flashed by in snatches as she wound down the spiral—sky, sky, sky, then stone as she reached the level of the rest of the castle. At last she spilled from the foot of the stairs into a gloomy room.

Before her stood a man holding two cups and a bottle of wine. He wore a dark jerkin and a cloak worked over with golden threads, and his beard was clipped into a neat point. Ellie felt all her blood rush to her head.

"Your Majesty?" said Lord de Lays. His voice was at once cordial and steely. "What are you doing out of your room? I was on my way to see you." He raised the cups. "I thought we might have a little chat about your future."

262   LEAGUE OF ARCHERS

Beneath Henry's red cloak, Ellie said nothing. Her hand, hidden in the half darkness, was on her bow.

Do I dare use it?

The baron squinted up at her. "Come now, back upstairs. The men I've charged with protecting you haven't done so well, have they? How shall we punish them, my king?"

Still Ellie said nothing. Her fingers were reaching for an arrow.

The baron frowned. "What is this silence? You've found nothing but respect in my home, where you are an esteemed guest. Come, let's take you back upstairs. I have friends arriving soon who are eager to meet you. They have come all the way from France for the honor. . . ."

"Henry's gone." Ellie's voice echoed around the room.

"What?" The baron's voice was a strangled whisper.

"The king is far away, and your plan has failed."

His face twisted. "Who *are* you?" he growled.

"One you made an outlaw." Ellie threw back the hood of her cloak. "I am Elinor Dray."

22

THE BARON'S FACE WENT PURPLE WITH RAGE. "I'll find the king!" he snarled. "There's nowhere you can hide him from me. I'll burn down every village and your precious Sherwood Forest before I let him get away. And you—I'll make sure you hang for this."

He moved closer, his hands working into fists as if he were imagining them around her throat. "But I won't show you the mercy I gave to your mother—no quick drop and a broken neck for Elinor Dray. You'll hang on a short rope, so I can watch you die slow."

Ellie's bow was drawn and an arrow nocked before the words faded away.

"It's over for you," she said, her voice steady and

certain. "Your cruelty and corruption have come to an end."

The baron grew very still. "You really do fancy yourself the next Robin Hood, don't you?" His voice was a mix of wonder and scorn. "But you see, Robin had a very bad habit of staying alive. I don't think I'll have the same problem with you."

With surprising speed he drew a dagger from his belt and hurled it at her. Ellie jumped back, onto the lowest stair, and it clattered onto the stone floor. The backs of her legs struck a stair and she fell. The baron leaped at her, sword drawn. With a gasp Ellie rolled clear. His blade slammed into the steps with a shower of white sparks.

"Stupid girl!" he bellowed.

Ellie scrambled back desperately—to have any chance of making a shot, she needed some distance to take aim. But he was already swinging again. She lunged aside, his sword slicing off a strip of the red cloak. She could sense the power in his blow. The baron was strong, there was no doubt about it.

So was Stephen, she reminded herself. *And I beat him.*

The baron roared and swung again. The sword ran through the cloak this time, pinning Ellie to the wall. She tore at the collar, ripping it away, and jumped free.

The baron was angry, and it was throwing him wide of his target. She knew it was all that was keeping her alive.

The baron's sword swung close, so close she felt the burning slide of its blade across her neck. She fell back, slamming so hard into the stone steps she couldn't breathe. The baron raised his sword over her, making ready to end the fight.

"You monstrous, unnatural girl," he snarled. "I should have killed you the day I took you from the abbey. I'm righting that wrong now—and don't worry, your friends will be joining you soon."

Ellie's hands moved restlessly, looking for something—anything—to beat him back with. Her fingers found the hilt of a blade—the dagger the baron had thrown to disarm her. She swung it awkwardly, catching the meat of his leg. He swore, staggering sideways. Ellie scrambled backward, but his heavy boot, now spattered in blood, pinned her in place.

"Prepare to die," the baron said, raising his sword over her once more.

A feeling like fever spread through Ellie's limbs. She'd never see Ralf again, or Marian. The breeze would never touch her face, and she wouldn't watch another sunrise.

"Our Father," she murmured, "who art in heaven . . ."

"Prayers will not save you now." The baron swung the

sword down. Ellie stiffened all over, braced for the final blow.

But the baron drew up, shrieking with pain. He slumped against the wall, his sword dropping harmlessly to his side. Jutting from his shoulder was an arrow.

In the gloom of the doorway was a boy—too tall to be Ralf, too thickset to be Jacob.

Stephen!

He stepped forward. The light caught his hair, making it burn like fire. He held his bow ready, a second arrow already set to the string.

"You," the baron said, his voice dripping with pain and poison. "You would betray me, boy?"

Stephen kept the arrow trained on his father. "Drop the sword," he said coolly. "Step away from Ellie and put your hands in the air."

The baron ignored his command. He put a hand to his shoulder, the fingers coming away bloody. "I should have known better than to believe you, you coward. You're nothing but a disappointment!"

"So you've told me a hundred times already." Stephen's blue eyes were cold as glass.

"You're choosing to help an outlaw over your own father?"

Stephen's lip curled. "*Really?* You claim me as your son

now? You could have done so when Mother died and I was all alone. Or when I came home from the war you sent me to. All I ever wanted was for you to be proud of me, and what have I got instead? You either ignore me or insult me."

"Of course you're my son." The baron's eyes were wild, flicking between Ellie, still crouched by the stairs, and Stephen in the doorway. "Don't you see you're committing a traitorous act? Just drop that bow and all will be forgiven."

"No," Stephen spat. "*You're* the traitor—you killed the king, kidnapped his rightful heir, and would have sold him to the French if we hadn't taken him. Do what I say or I'll shoot you. Your blood runs through my veins, remember, so you know I mean it."

The baron dropped his sword.. He raised his arms above his head, wincing with pain. His expression was murderous.

"Ellie? Can you stand?"

She got to her feet, her limbs trembling all over with relief. She slid past the baron and hurried to Stephen's side.

"Turn around, Father." The baron did so and Stephen carefully withdrew the bloody arrow, then threw it aside. "Now walk up the stairs."

Slowly, radiating rage, the baron did as he was told. Stephen kept the tip of his arrow poking into his back as they wound back up. Ellie followed close behind, her own bow ready in case.

"I have always been proud to call you my son," the baron said as they climbed. "I admit I was perhaps a little stern, but I had your best interests—"

"Shut your mouth and walk faster."

When they reached Henry's cell, the baron paused on the threshold. "What are you going to do with me?" For the first time he looked properly afraid.

"Don't worry, Father. I'll treat you with far more mercy than you've ever shown me. Ellie, watch him."

Ellie kept her arrow trained on the baron as Stephen stripped the linens from the king's bed. He directed his father to sit on the room's plainest chair, then tied his hands behind it with a strip of bedsheet. Once they were secured, he and Ellie used the bit of uncut rope left from her climb into the tower to tie him tightly in place. The chair they lashed to the leg of a heavy dresser. The baron looked smaller than she'd ever seen him, a foolish tyrant diminished by his fear.

"You call this mercy?" the baron asked, an edge of panic in his voice. "Leaving me here to die?"

Stephen smiled tightly. "But you'll be in these fine

chambers, where the king was made your guest!" Then the smile dropped. He knelt in front of the baron and spat the next words into his face. "If I did *kill* you, it wouldn't be punishment enough for all your crimes. So it's lucky I'm not you, isn't it? We share the same blood, but really I'm very different. I'm going to let you live. But you'll stay here until the king is safely away."

The baron started to retort, but Stephen cut him off by tying his scarf tightly around his father's mouth.

"Come on," Stephen said to Ellie, his face suddenly weary. "Let's go."

They went back down the stairs and into the room where Stephen had appeared. "Where's the king?" Ellie asked as they turned into a narrow passageway.

"He's safe for the time being. Even safer now my father's out of the way."

Ellie sneaked a look at Stephen's face. He was glaring ahead, his jaw set, as if he still had his father in his sights. She gave him a nudge. "Thank you. For saving my life."

Stephen shook himself, managed a half smile. "Thank *you*. I know that if I'd done this before I met you, I would've killed him. But I'm glad I didn't. I tried it your way. I've done . . . well, I've done my share of bad deeds. It's about time I made amends, don't you think?"

She remembered what Marian had told her. "Everyone

deserves a chance, Stephen. Make sure you give yourself one."

He squeezed her hand, so briefly she wondered if she'd imagined it.

"So are you glad now that you let me join the League of Archers?" Some of the old swagger crept back into his voice. "It took a while, but it paid off eventually."

Ellie laughed. "Yes. I suppose it did."

23

AS THEY MADE THEIR WAY BACK OUT TO THE courtyard, Stephen filled Ellie in on what had happened while she was trapped in the tower. "I fetched a horse and met the rest of the League outside, like I said I would. But then I saw them fighting—your friends versus my father's men." He pushed open a door, ushered her through it. "I thought the worst—that Father's soldiers were trying to take back the king. But Ralf told me you were stuck in the tower, and they were trying to give you a chance of getting out. So I went to see if I could help. And that's how I found you. Fighting *him*."

"You mean about to be killed by him." She stopped short as they passed a huge window with views onto the hillside that stretched beyond the tower. Something glittering had caught her eye.

"What is it?"

"Oh," Ellie breathed. "Look."

Coming over the hillside, armor shining in the late sun, a vast regiment was marching on the castle.

Stephen swore. "It's the French, it must be. Coming to collect Henry."

Guilt seized Ellie's guts. Henry should be long gone, riding with Stephen and the League toward the safety of Maid Marian and the Greenwood Tree. Instead they'd stayed to save her. "Your father's plan—it could still work!"

"We won't let it," Stephen said grimly. "We can't. If France gets hold of England's heir, France gets hold of *England*. Who knows what kind of power they've promised my father in return?"

They ran the rest of the way, bursting into the courtyard. It was a mass of brawling bodies—soldiers, servants, guards, all of them fighting with whatever they had.

"There they are!" Stephen grabbed her arm and pulled her toward the center of the fight, where the League stood in tight formation. Backs in and weapons out, they defended themselves against a knot of the baron's men.

A soldier with a blond beard was laughing at Alice, half his size and swiping at him viciously with her knife.

"Look at the little girl go," he yelled at his friends—then screamed as she sliced him with a shallow gash beneath the armpit. Before he could strike back, Ellie shot an arrow into his arm, firing as she ran toward her friends. Relief colored her friends' faces when they saw her, just briefly, before they were absorbed by the battle again. Behind Jacob, shielded from attack, was Henry, still clutching the cloak around his face.

But did the guards know who he was? She wasn't sure. All she knew was that the League had started this brawl for her, and now they couldn't get clear of it. She fired another arrow, reloaded.

"Stop," Stephen cried, grabbing the arm of the guard menacing Jacob. "Stop fighting these . . . these *peasants*, and start getting the rest of them under control! That's an order!"

"We need to go," Ellie said when she reached Ralf. "The French troops are on their way—we need to get Henry away from the castle now!"

"These aren't no peasants," one of the guards said to Stephen in an ugly, coarse voice. "These are the League of Archers! Your *friends*."

"In the name of my father," Stephen growled, "stand down."

Another guard sneered at him. "We take orders from

Lord de Lays, not his runaway son. There'll be a reward from the baron for capturing the League of Archers—and a bigger one for recapturing the king!"

They know. . . .

Ellie saw the dangerous change in the other soldiers' faces at his words. A few of them had looked uncertain when they saw Stephen, but the promise of money—the kind you get when you take down a band of outlaws and reclaim a kidnapped king—had made up their minds.

She hurried back a few paces until she was at range to use her longbow. The rest of the brawlers started to quiet, all of them realizing now what they were seeing in the center of the courtyard: the baron's men fighting the legendary League of Archers.

Stephen, realizing that his orders were useless, struck at the man who'd shouted him down, blade singing. Margery mirrored Ellie on the other side, wielding her bow to strike where her friends most needed her. Ellie shot arrow after arrow, barely pausing to check where her shots fell, disarming the baron's men and beating them back from hurting the rest of the League—or Stephen, who'd downed one guard and was fighting a second.

Alice screamed as the blond-bearded guard took her under his arm in a choke hold. Ellie stopped him with an arrow just below his throat, serious enough to scare him, but not deadly. Alice rolled free and came up in a crouch, driving her knife into the leg of a man who'd just punched Ralf to the ground. A man who'd lost his weapon was fighting hand to hand with Jacob, who kept swiping at him with a stolen shield, still trying to keep Henry behind him.

Ellie reached for another arrow and found that just one remained: The stolen silver arrow rattled lonely in her quiver. She nocked it to her bow and ran to Jacob's side to help defend the king.

A hunting horn split the air. Everyone turned toward it. Over the drawbridge came galloping a legion of knights in glistening armor, filling the courtyard with shouts and steaming horses.

Too late. The French were here to take Henry.

The League had failed. Ellie had failed.

And when the king was taken and the baron freed, what would happen to them all?

We'll go down fighting, that's what. She raised the silver arrow, steeling herself to end the first person who tried to lay a hand on Henry.

But when she glanced back at the king, he was no longer hiding behind Jacob. His hood was thrown back. And he was . . . smiling.

So was Ralf. He grabbed her arm. "Look, Ellie! Look at what they're carrying!"

Over the knights' heads colorful standards whipped in the air. They bore three lions on a scarlet background. Ellie gasped. It was the royal coat of arms and these were King John's knights.

No, not King John's anymore. King Henry's.

The soldiers surrounding the League fell nervously away. Ellie spotted two familiar figures riding with the knights on a pair of dark horses—Friar Tuck and Maid Marian.

"We're here!" Ellie called to them. "And the king is safe!"

Marian leaped gracefully from her horse's back and plunged through the throng to Ellie. Her eyes shone and she clasped Ellie tightly to her chest. "I didn't doubt you and the League could save the king on your own," she said, "but William Marshall thought you might need some help. We rode to Nottingham for the king's forces."

"I'm so glad you did!"

A pure-white charger cantered through the knights. On it rode a woman in a blue velvet cloak. Her oval face was framed with long brown ringlets and topped by a small golden crown. "Henri!" she cried in a French accent, sliding down from her horse, her arms thrown open wide.

The young king gave a wordless cry and ran into her

embrace, burying his face into her neck. For the first time he looked as young as he had that first day, when Ellie opened the door to his coach.

Alice was gawping at the lady. "Who is she?"

"Queen Isabella," Marian said. "Henry's mother."

"And she's still got her circlet," said Ralf, grinning at Ellie.

Queen Isabella released her hold on Henry and touched his bandaged arm. "Is the hurt bad?"

Henry shook his head. "I'm fine, Mama. Far worse would have happened if not for my new friends." Then he was leading the queen by the hand toward Ellie and the League of Archers.

A hush had fallen over the courtyard. A number of the castle servants knelt as the queen walked past them. The soldiers took off their helmets and bowed their heads. Ellie felt her friends gather behind her, suddenly wondering how she should greet a queen.

Isabella stood before them. All the songs were right, Ellie thought: The queen was beautiful, even more so than she'd seemed from afar. Her eyes were gray and serious, and red at the corners in a way that made Ellie think of her own mother—she must have passed sleepless nights worrying about her son. Her skin was as smooth and fair as fresh cream.

LEAGUE OF ARCHERS

Ellie dipped into an awkward curtsy. Alice and Margery did the same, while the boys bowed.

"These are my friends, Mama," Henry said eagerly. "They're outlaws who fight back against injustice and try to take care of the poor. They're brave and good, and they live without blankets or walls in the woods. And they saved me from Lord de Lays."

Ellie found herself blushing. Who would have thought a lowly ex-novice would receive such praise from a king?

Henry beamed at his mother. "They're called the League of Archers."

24

QUEEN ISABELLA SMILED, HER EYES FILLED with warmth. "Your good deeds have reached even my ears," she said, her accent rolling the words musically. "I heard that you were young, but I did not think . . ."

She lifted a hand, indicating that they should rise. Ellie could feel hundreds of pairs of eyes upon them.

Queen Isabella moved closer, as if she were going to tell them a secret, then spoke loud enough for everyone to hear. "I can never repay you for what you've done," the queen said. "For saving the king. Saving my *son*. Not just his life, but countless others that would have been lost to civil war if the baron's plans had succeeded."

Henry put a hand on her sleeve; she leaned down so he

could speak in her ear. When she straightened, she leveled her gaze on Ellie.

"Henri tells me you're the leader of this League of Archers."

Ellie cleared her throat. "I am, Your Majesty."

"What's your name?"

"Dray," Ellie said, curtsying again. "Elinor Dray."

The queen raised her hands to her head. Carefully she lifted the golden circlet from her hair and laid it in Ellie's hands. Ellie didn't think she'd seen anything lovelier— it was made of three bands of gold, intricately wrapped around one another, glowing in the chilly sunlight. She looked up at Isabella, wondering why she'd given it to her.

"The bishops await us in Gloucester," the queen said, "where my son will be crowned king. But these last few weeks I've learned it can be dangerous to wait. Let us put everything in order now. Elinor Dray, will you do us the honor of crowning our new king?"

Margery gasped. The rest of the League was grinning, watching Ellie with round eyes. Ellie flushed hot and nodded, wishing fiercely, more than she had in years, that her parents were alive. That they were here to see this: their daughter, in a muddy courtyard on a cold day, with the queen of England's crown in her hands, the country's new king before her.

Ellie saw her breath mist the air, smelled the ordinary smells of sweat and dung and mud, and knew she would remember this day until she died. All who hadn't dropped to their knees did so now—Tuck and Marian, the League. Guards and soldiers and servants. Stephen. Last of all the queen herself. Only Ellie and Henry stood in a sea of bowed heads.

The young king's face was solemn and shining. After a long, charged moment he grinned. She grinned back and stepped forward. He stood proud and straight as she carefully placed the crown on his head.

"God save the king!" cried Friar Tuck's baritone. "God save King Henry!"

The whole courtyard seemed to exhale. Suddenly everyone was cheering and scrambling to their feet, people dabbing sleeves and aprons to their eyes, turning to embrace their neighbors. Ralf's arm was around Ellie's shoulder, pulling her into a hug.

At length Henry raised a hand, and quiet spread through the crowd. "As your king," he said, "I make my first proclamation: The League of Archers are hereby pardoned. Maid Marian and Friar Tuck, too! They are no longer outlaws, or enemies to the Crown. The families sheltering in Sherwood Forest are free to stay there—or to return to their homes— whichever they choose. They are under my protection."

Joy rose in Ellie like water bubbling up from some hidden source. Her friends' stunned, happy faces mirrored her own.

"We did it," Alice said in a low, unsteady voice, like she couldn't believe it. "It's all because of *you*, Ellie. You're the one who saved the king."

"It was all of us," Ellie replied. "Always."

A commotion stirred at the other side of the courtyard. "Get your hands off me before I remove them myself!" came the baron's furious voice. He was dragged before Henry, struggling, between two of the king's men. His eyes were lit with rage, but the fire went out of them when he saw Henry wearing the circlet, Queen Isabella beside him.

"Lord de Lays." Henry's voice was quiet, but it cut like a knife. "What should I do with you? You kidnapped me. You plotted to hand me over to France. You drove people from their homes, you taxed them into your dungeons or the grave, and you gorged yourself while they starved." Henry's head dropped a little, as if he suddenly felt the full weight of his crown. "For your crimes you deserve a traitor's punishment."

The color drained from the baron's face. He sagged forward and the two knights had to hold him upright.

The traitor's punishment, Ellie knew, was death.

"Wait!" It was Stephen, pushing through the crowd. He stepped between his father and the king and dropped to one knee. "Your Majesty, my father's crimes are great. But I beg you to show him mercy. To give him . . . a second chance." He glanced at Ellie, caught her gaze. "People can change if you let them. I should know."

Henry looked from Stephen to the baron, his eyes thoughtful. "I know what it is to have a bad father," he said. "Everyone here knows what King John was like. But I cannot allow Lord de Lays to go unpunished."

Panic flashed across Stephen's face. "Please, I beg—"

"But I will not order his death. Not for his sake, but for yours. And mine—I've been king barely a minute and would rather show mercy today."

Stephen let out a long breath.

"But I'm taking his title away," said Henry. He turned to the baron, whose cheeks were starting to fill with color. "From this day forth you'll be no more a baron than the poorest soul in your dungeons—which will today be emptied. Take my mercy and leave. You are forbidden to ever set foot on English soil again." A smile ghosted over his lips. "Perhaps the French king will have you. You have always been a friend to him."

The knights holding the baron loosened their grip. The baron stumbled into the dirt, then regained his feet.

He looked around ferociously. "A horse—bring me my horse!"

Nobody responded, not even the baron's groom, who stood watching from the crowd. Finally the baron shoved through the throng of people and grabbed the bridle of the horse Stephen had readied to carry the king away. He pulled himself onto the saddle, wheeled around, then rode hard over the drawbridge. Not once did he thank his son for pleading for his life or even look back at him.

King Henry and Queen Isabella moved away, quietly conferring. The knights began mounting their horses. Chatter broke out through the courtyard once more, the League of Archers grinning and talking together.

Stephen stood apart from them all. Ellie went over. He blinked hastily and drew a sleeve over his eyes.

"You know what," Ellie said, "I think I just about feel proud of you. A really tiny bit."

"Really?"

"You did it, didn't you? You proved that you're better than your father."

"If you say so. It's not hard to improve on him, but it's a start. I'm hoping I'll do a better job."

Ellie looked up at him. "Wait—does this mean you're now Lord de Lays?"

Stephen nodded. "I can hardly believe it either, but

yes—I started today an outlaw and ended it a baron." Some of the gleam returned to his blue eyes. "And I've got a first proclamation of my own—the League of Archers can hunt on my land whenever they wish."

Ellie grinned. He turned on his heel and went to talk to some of the soldiers and servants. The king and queen mounted their horses and rode to the head of their cadre of knights. The two royals circled the courtyard slowly, reaching their hands down to those stretched up from the crowd. As they rode onto the drawbridge, Henry looked back over his shoulder and gave a final wave toward Ellie, crown glittering. She waved back and watched until he and his retinue had disappeared from view.

The League had gathered around her. Ralf nodded toward where Stephen was bossing around the soldiers. Stephen jabbed a finger at the guard who'd told him off. "From now on the runaway son's in charge! Do you understand me?"

"The new Lord de Lays," Ralf said. "Saints preserve us."

Alice rolled her eyes. "I wonder what life will be like under this new baron."

Jacob eyed Stephen doubtfully. "Not easy, I would guess."

"But I think better than it was," Ellie said. "We've taught Stephen a thing or two."

286

"Maybe," said Ralf. "Let's wait a few weeks before we decide about that."

Ellie threw an arm around his shoulders. "It can't do us any harm to have a new baron who has fought beside the League of Archers—and a new king who has done the same! Things are bound to get better now, aren't they?"

"Definitely," Margery said firmly.

"So what now?" wondered Alice. "Back to the Greenwood Tree?"

Ellie suddenly realized it was what she wanted more than anything. The villagers would be able to return home now, and all would be as it was before—just the five of them, with Marian and Tuck visiting when they weren't on the road. She couldn't wait.

"Yes," she said, half to herself. "Let's go home."

Marian and Tuck were already making their way to the drawbridge. The League were close behind when Stephen caught up with them.

"Wait!" he said. "You're not leaving, are you?"

Ellie nodded.

"Look, why don't you stay? I can give you places in my household, anything you want. Jacob, you can be the castle fletcher, of course. Margery, you can be the farrier—you're good with horses. Ellie, you'd be captain of the guard!"

Ellie couldn't help but be touched by his eagerness. But she shook her head. "I don't think the guards would like that much."

Stephen waved a hand, dismissing this. "Who cares? It's my castle."

Alice opened her mouth in retort and Ellie hastily spoke over her. "Thank you, but no," she said. "Our place isn't here. We belong at the Greenwood Tree. After all, your father wasn't the only bad baron. There are more villages that need our help."

"The Sheriff of Nottingham won't be happy your father's gone," Ralf added.

"And besides," Ellie said, "you're a baron now yourself. You'll need the League of Archers watching over you, to make sure you remember the right way to rule."

Stephen flashed one of his most brilliant smiles. He gave Ellie a courtly bow. "I look forward to being kept in line. Until we meet again, Elinor Dray."

"A husband? Mary Ursula has gone to France to look for a *husband*?" Ellie set down her mug of hot milk on the abbey's kitchen table and laughed until tears came into her eyes. First Sister Bethan, then Sisters Joan and Agnes, joined her, till all four were nearly crying.

"You should've seen her out of her habit," Sister

Bethan gasped. "Wearing a fine gown and proud as a peacock!"

Sister Agnes dabbed her eyes. "It isn't right to mock her . . . but she soaked her hair in ale and honey for a day before she went, hoping to make it yellow!"

"She'll be attracting far more wasps than men if those are her tactics," Sister Joan said.

Sister Bethan collected herself, patting Ellie's hand fondly. "It's because you sent the baron to ground like a rabbit. She was on her way quick after that. She knew she wouldn't last long without him to prop her up."

"She's going to tell the men in France she's a wealthy widow," Sister Agnes said primly. "I heard her telling Sister Muriel."

"Well, I feel sorry for the men of France," said Sister Joan.

Ellie remembered the piles of splendid things heaped in Mary Ursula's room when she was the mother abbess, the hard glitter of them in the dark—and she had a thought that made her eyes go wide. She tucked it away for later.

"Tomorrow you'll have a new abbess," she said, smiling slyly at Sister Bethan. "And I think I know who will be chosen."

"Anything can happen in an election," Sister Bethan said, flushing.

"And yet we all know it will be you," Sister Joan replied warmly. "And none could deserve it more."

Ellie lifted her mug. "To the rightful abbess of Kirklees, finally taking her place."

Sister Agnes tapped her mug to Ellie's, then dissolved into laughter again. "I can't stop seeing her," she gasped, "with her head all covered in honey!"

Ellie listened to the nuns chatter on. She'd spent many hours in this kitchen when she was very young. Here she'd been an orphan, grieving and alone. Here she'd become Sister Bethan's small shadow, keeping close to the sister she loved best and learning to bake bread. Here she'd been a novice with a secret, slipping out the kitchen door and into the woods beyond the wall, to hunt the baron's game with her best friends.

And sitting here now, she was happier than she'd ever been. The baron was too far away to hurt anyone she loved. All was well at the nunnery and would be for many years with Sister Bethan running things. The League of Archers were reunited, and even closer than before.

Just one more thing to do, she thought.

25

THE SEA WAS BIGGER THAN ANYTHING IN THE world. It went on and on forever, until it met the sky miles away. It was just as endless as the sky, and just as changeable. It was blue and green and gray, purple in the distance, white where the water crested into foamy caps, then lapped against the rocks of King's Lynn port. This was Ellie's first sight of it and she was transfixed. She sat on the sand, breathing in the tangy smell of fish and salt.

Ralf and Alice were ankle-deep in the water, grabbing pebbles from the beach and sending them skimming across the water. Margery squealed as another wave rolled in, the cold water breaking around her legs. A little way out a cluster of ships was moored at the end of the docks. Ellie watched them, restless, wondering when Jacob would be back from his lookout post.

Ralf whooped as one of his stones went hopping across the water, touching down five times before it sank. They'd arrived the night before, and a sailor they met on the beach had taught him the trick. "Did you see that?" he called to Ellie.

"The best one yet!" she called back.

Ralf waded in to sit next to her. "Are you sure this is the right place?" he asked. "We've been waiting a long time. Maybe we should go back to the inn, have more oysters. . . ."

"I'm sure," Ellie said firmly. "You know what Friar Tuck's like for gossip. Their carriage has been spotted on the road here more than once. They've got to be—"

"They're coming!" It was Jacob, pelting down from the road, his cloak flapping behind him. "They're almost here!"

Ellie grabbed her bow. "Margery! Alice! It's time!"

They hurried away from the beach, Alice, Margery, and Ralf with sandy bare feet, and made their way to the main road that entered King's Lynn. The nearby docks were thronged with boats and sailors, but the road itself was quiet and rolled through a flat, scrubby landscape. No one was around, Ellie noted with satisfaction, as they hid behind a large gorse bush, weapons at the ready. The carriage was already close, its paintwork shabby, pulled along by two gray ponies. An equally gray man was driving it.

When it was a few paces away, Ellie sprang to her feet. She stepped out into the road and leveled her bow at the driver. His eyes widened, but before he could raise the alarm, she lowered the arrow and put a finger to her lips. Ralf joined her, waving a bag of coins at the man.

He drew the carriage to a halt, got down, and whistled softly when Ralf tossed him the bag of coins. "I'll be on my way, then," he said in a low voice, and set off toward the town.

Quietly the League surrounded the coach, arrows drawn. When Ellie got close enough, the burr of conversation from within sharpened into two distinct voices: one a woman's wheedling tones, the other the arrogant sniping of a man.

"You and that ridiculous gown have taken up altogether too much room on this journey."

"Oh, you think my gown's ridiculous? Was it really necessary for you to travel with six busts of yourself? That's truly ridiculous. Could you not have sold them in Nottingham?"

"There was a time when many would've paid good

money for my likeness," the man replied querulously. "But let's talk of more important things—like the jewels. I'll gladly give you this bust if you agree that I will have the emeralds."

"The emeralds!" the woman squawked. Her voice went high and lofty. "Emeralds symbolize the glory of God and all his saints. Naturally, the emeralds must stay with me."

The man spoke through gritted teeth. "Of course that is so, but if you consider that—"

"Wait. Why aren't we moving?"

The man's indignation grew. "That fool driver must think we're paying him by the hour." A rapping came from within the coach. "Driver! Old man, answer me!"

Worried she'd burst out laughing if she waited any longer, Ellie threw open the door of the coach.

Inside, the former Lord de Lays and Mary Ursula froze, blinking in the sudden light. The two looked half-buried in finery and bags stuffed, Ellie knew, with the abbey's treasures. Mary Ursula screamed and de Lays spluttered with fury.

"Hello, Master de Lays, Mistress Mary Ursula," Ellie said pleasantly. Their much-reduced positions felt delicious on her tongue. The League fanned out behind her, each training an arrow on the interior of the carriage.

"You little *flea*," Master de Lays spat. "Always hopping around. Always destroying my happiness. Always a cursed nuisance!"

Mary Ursula smacked his arm. "This is your fault! You should have gotten rid of her when you had the chance." She folded her pale lips together tightly and glared at Ellie. "What do you want?"

Ellie smiled at her. "The crown jewels, if you please."

Mary Ursula gasped. For a moment de Lays looked as if he might charge at Ellie, despite the League's arrows. His face quivered with rage as he realized how hopeless his situation was, and he pointed to a sack tucked next to his feet.

"They're here," he growled.

"Hand them over, then," Ellie said cheerfully. "You'll forgive me if I don't trust you enough to reach in there myself."

He lifted the sack and dumped it into her outstretched arms. Ellie nearly staggered with the weight of it. The mouth of the sack slid open, revealing a heap of treasures topped with a glittering crown embedded with jewels. She couldn't help grinning.

"Wow," breathed Margery. Their bows still in place, the League peered at the loot the former baron had nearly carried away to France.

Mary Ursula snuffled into a lace handkerchief. "How did you know?" de Lays demanded of Ellie.

"Crown jewels don't just disappear," Ellie said, handing the sack over to Alice. "And the treasure I saw in Mary Ursula's chambers was far too fine to belong at Kirklees. Besides, Master de Lays, I knew from the beginning that you were behind this. Wherever there's trouble, you're always there. Or you used to be."

She stepped back and bowed.

"Enjoy France, sir. And I wish you good fortune in your husband hunting, Mary Ursula."

And she slammed the carriage door shut, hoping never to see either of their faces again.

Laughing, the League ran back up the road to where they'd tied their horses, leaving the carriage behind. They took to the road on foot, leading the horses, the sea behind them and the countryside ahead. Once their laughter had died down, Alice looked at Ellie narrowly. "We're not giving the crown jewels back to Henry, are we?"

"What kind of outlaws would that make us?" said Ellie. "Henry's a good king, but he'll be an even better one if he's got subjects who can fight back. If we've got money, we can fight. And maybe we'll need to build our farm one day, to help other villagers escape barons who take more than they should. These jewels mean we can do that."

"I don't think Henry would mind us keeping them," said Jacob.

"Me neither," said Margery.

They walked shoulder to shoulder on the road. Already the seaside scrub was giving way to green leaves and rich brown earth.

"But these jewels make us rich, don't they?" said Ralf forlornly. "Between that and the king's pardon, we're not really outlaws at all."

"I'm still an outlaw," Alice said fiercely, touching her fingertips to the scar on her cheek. "A rich man's pardon doesn't change that."

Ellie linked one arm through Alice's and the other through Ralf's. "We're still outlaws," she said, "and we always will be, because those jewels aren't really ours. We've stolen them from the rich to give to the poor."

Ralf grinned at her. "Like Robin Hood."

"Yes," said Ellie, smiling back at him. "Just like Robin Hood."

The setting sun threw their five shadows long across the road as the League of Archers made their way to Sherwood Forest.

ABOUT THE AUTHOR

When she's not writing, Eva Howard escapes the city to hike and camp in the forest—and has even tried her hand at archery. She lives in New York.